Flashpoint

Frank Myers

A Black Horse Western

ROBERT HALE · LONDON

© 1966, 2002 John Glasby
First hardcover edition 2002
Originally published in paperback as
Guns at Rimrock by Chuck Adams

ISBN 0 7090 7217 1

Robert Hale Limited
Clerkenwell House
Clerkenwell Green
London EC1R 0HT

Typeset by
Derek Doyle & Associates, Liverpool.
Printed and bound in Great Britain by
Antony Rowe Limited, Wiltshire

ONE

RIMROCK

It was an hour after high noon and from the rimrock, Dave Tremaine looked down into the valley that lay spread out beneath him in the blistering heat. The sun was a furnace that blazed down from a cloudless sky and even here, some three hundred feet above the valley floor there was no breeze to mitigate the fierce glare. A cloud of buzzards wheeled in lazy circles against the vivid blue-white of the heavens, gazing with a patient hope at the man who sat forward in his saddle, his hat pushed over his forehead.

The trail led down into the vast depression where long rocky gulches and dense thickets of chapparal made it wind around like the hind leg of a dog, sometimes losing itself in thorn and mesquite. He had ridden for fourteen heat-filled days, gradually edging his way across the Badlands. This, he knew, was the narrow middle of them, the waist of the desert, squeezed in between the Big Smoky and the Yellow Rivers. Far off, to the north. he could just make out the rising summits of tall mountains, shimmering in a purpling of sun-haze on the skyline.

Tremaine's grey eyes flickered as he scanned the unfriendly country that lay ahead of him. He was a big man in every way; tall and loose-limbed, sitting the saddle with a rider's easiness. He had a gun on his left hip, the smoothly-oiled holster low down since he was a long-armed man. Under the black, flat-crowned sombrero, his features were etched in shadow, the aquiline nose and high cheekbones outlining the sun-browned face. All of his features were solid and his shape was the lean, whip-hard figure of a man who lived by the horse and the gun. Yet there was something about his face, about the look in the eyes perhaps, that marked him out from most men. Such was the expression on the faces of men following a vengeance trail, intent on running a man to earth and getting him on the wrong end of a gun.

The black sorrel was restless, pawed at the earth with its forelegs, seemed anxious to move on. Tremaine watched the ears twitch for a few moments, then relaxed his tight-fisted hold on the reins, let it pick its own way down the stony slope. Although the two rivers bordered this stretch of the Badlands, lying at their narrowest less than fifteen miles apart, there was no water in the desert itself, though some of the old-timers who had prospected this place many years before still asserted that there were springs and hidden water holes if one cared to take the trouble to look for them.

Tremaine's lips stretched into a thin travesty of a smile. He guessed that nobody cared to venture here anyway and certainly nobody wanted to spend any time there exploring the territory. It was a dangerous place for anyone, the hideout for men on the run, men keeping one jump ahead of the law, the wild ones who preyed on anyone passing through.

Moving leisurely down a narrow trail that angled so sharply in places that only the sure-footedness of his mount kept them from sliding all the way to the valley floor, he arrived at length to a levelling-off place where huge boulders, etched by wind and scouring sand into fantastic shapes, lay strewn over the rocky ground. The ledge was composed mainly of rock and dirt, with very little vegetation clinging to it. At times, it pulled close against the bare rock of the cliff with the face of a precipice tumbling away at a breakneck angle, dropping for almost a hundred feet before it reached the jumble of boulders at the bottom. But the sorrel was a sure-footed beast and past experience on similar trails had made him cautious and wary. He moved gently, with mincing steps until they were at the bottom, then put his mount forward, touching spurs to its flanks, anxious to be on the move as quickly as possible.

It was nearly four o'clock in the afternoon as he came to the furthermost edge of the valley. It had stretched longer than he had thought and the heat on his back and shoulders was a burning pressure, a shimmering that shocked up from the burnt-out sage that grew alongside the winding trail, scenting the air with its arid smell. His body ached with the heat and he realized that he was riding low in the saddle, that even the horse had its head bowed between its forelegs. With an effort, he straightened himself, stared out in front of him, narrowing his eyes down to mere slits in the face of the great yellow-white glare from the weltering sun.

There was a long line of buttes in the distance. He had noticed them a couple of hours earlier from halfway along the valley floor. They stood out prominently now on the western horizon, with the sunlight glinting off their serrated tops and he reckoned they were about half a dozen miles further on. The Smoky River would lie somewhere beyond them, he estimated. He had made this his destination for the evening, wondered now if he would reach it before dark.

Pushing the broad-brimmed hat back on his head a little, he rubbed his forehead with his fingers, where the sweat had plastered the hair tightly down against his scalp and the rim of the hat had rubbed an angry red weal in the flesh.

Twice, during the days he had been on the trail, he had seen riders in the distance, tiny puffs of trail-smoke on the skyline, angling along a different trail to that which he followed. On occasion too, he had come upon narrow

trails in the thick forests on the tall mountain slopes, trails
which had too obviously led to some shack well off the
beaten trail. He had ignored them all, even when the
smell of brushsmoke had drifted down to him from the
green fastnesses. The men in this part of the territory
chose to remain apart from their fellows deliberately, did
not take kindly to strangers riding in on them.

This country was sparsely inhabited, a lawless land
where for every man it was a question of struggling to
survive against a bitter nature which wanted nothing of
men. As was usual in such circumstances, the strongest
and most ruthless survived at the expense of others and
the law of the sixgun ruled supreme.

Gradually the country began to lift again from its
rolling flatness. The buttes were ahead of him now, atop
the low hills and the lowering sun threw long, black shadows over the red sandstone desert, lighting it with an
ochreous flame. The trail was a yellow streak and ran
straight as a die now through a narrow pass between two
of the tall, upstanding butts. There seemed to be no movement at all in this arid, barren land, apart from the occasional skitter of a purple-and-green lizard as it darted from
one concealing rock to another, or the smoothly sinuous
movement of a rattler, disturbed by his passing, gliding
from a patch of vegetation. This was a land of huge rocks
and red boulders standing at the end of long shadows that
were curiously black and ominous, some hanging on the
edges of steep-sided precipices, balanced there precari-
ously, looking as if the slightest breath of wind would be
enough to tip them over the edge and send them crashing
down on to the trail. His own shadow ran behind him now
as the sun dipped lower and lower towards the buttes.
Ahead of him lay a long, narrow valley that led straight to
the pass and he could feel the evening's coolness flow
against his sun-burned face as he rode into it, the walls of
rock rising up on either side of him, shutting him in from
the outside world. The muffled sound of his mount's
hooves on the hard-packed dirt came echoing faintly back

at him from the rocks. As if sensing the presence of water somewhere in the near distance, the sorrel increased its pace, head lifted a little now and he patted its neck as he bent forward.

'Nearly there,' he said softly. 'Not much further to go now.'

The sun dropped behind the line of the buttes and the land around him was now blue and grey, with the distant smell of vegetation growing along the river reaching him. Black and bulky and high, the buttes lifted in front of him, great shadows of stone and as he rode through them he caught the tremendous immensity of them, crushing down on him from all sides. They created the impression of a vast pit, surrounded on all four sides by the colour-banded cliffs that rose in a sheer sweep to the sky's blue-and-gold emptiness.

The sun was down below the rim of the distant western horizon by the time he rode down from the pass into the plains which lay beyond, but he judged that there were still three hours or so clear daylight before it became too dark to see the trail. He did not intend to stop and make camp until he reached the river, but when he encountered a small cluster of stunted trees that grew a short distance from the trail, he wheeled the sorrel to the right, reined up and dismounted. There was time to rest himself and his horse before he continued on his way to the river, he decided. There was a little of the tough, springy grass growing around the trunks of the trees and he loosened the cinches, removed the heavy bit to allow the horse to graze more comfortably and went over to a small rock, seating himself on the flat top, pulling out his tobacco pouch and making himself a cigarette. He had no fear of the sorrel moving away; the horse had been well trained, obeyed his every command.

Drawing the sweet-smelling smoke deeply into his lungs, he gave himself up to reflection. Taking out the carefully folded piece of paper from his pocket, he smoothed it out flat on his knee, read through the words slowly, not that he needed to, for he had already read it so often that he knew it off by heart. The neat lines of writing said:

> *Just made my strike, Dave, and it's a bonanza. Somewhere to the north of Fenton in Texas. You remember the place. Just a few mud huts when we last rode through it. You wouldn't know the town now, since they found the gold in the hills. Railroad's come to Fenton too. Bringing big trouble though. I'd like you to come out soon as possible. Need somebody fast with a gun. Plenty of men trying to move in and squeeze us out.*
> *Clem.*

Tremaine stared fixedly at the letter for several minutes, then refolded it and thrust it back into his pocket. Frowning, he tried to recall the last time he had ridden through Fenton with Clem Fordyce. It must have been the best part of nine years before, he reckoned. Face taut, the memory was a slow acid burning deep within his brain, and the tightness grew within him, knotting the muscles of his stomach and chest. He had written three letters to Clem after receiving this one, had even wired him at Fenton, but there had been no reply to any of them and the feeling that something had happened to the oldster was something which had grown stronger with every day, until now it had crystallized into a virtual certainty.

If events had followed the course they so often did after gold was found near a small township, he could guess at what Fenton must be like now. Bringing the railroad there would open up that part of the territory and not only prospectors would move in on the place. There would be the usual horde of gamblers, killers, saloon keepers and dancing girls; hard-eyed men and women who cared for nothing but power and money. By now, Fenton would be a helltown, set on its own trail to perdition and damnation. Small wonder that Clem had been sufficiently worried to send for him, to ask for the help of a man who was fast with a gun.

Finishing his smoke, he dropped the glowing stub of the cigarette on to the sand and ground it out with his heel. Getting lithely to his feet, he walked over to his horse, tightened the cinch, placed the bit back between the animal's teeth and mounted up, throwing one quick look about him before riding out. The trail led him down through ground that grew steadily more proliferous, with many different kinds of vegetation springing up on all sides. Spanish sword predominated most of the way until he came within sight of the river, when it gave way, reluctantly it seemed, to a tough but green grass that grew almost knee deep along the banks of the river. Presumably this kind of country spread for several miles along the banks of the river and on the far side, stretching towards the hills far off in the distance, where he knew Fenton to lie in the small hollow beside a narrow tributary of the Smoky, there would be plenty of lush pasture for herds of prime beef cattle. That brought another thought to his mind and he turned it over in his head as he rode slowly through the deep blue and purple dusk. Once range men moved in on a small town that was in the process of growing up, they brought their own kinds of trouble with them; unscrupulous, ruthless land barons, anxious to build up their herds and their spreads at the expense of their neighbours, and none of these cattle men would have anything in common with the townsfolk, except hatred. Tremaine did not let that prospect worry him. He would be riding into Fenton for only one thing, to discover what had happened to Clem Fordyce. Depending on what he found there, would depend his actions.

The moon, a little before full, was rising above the distant end of the tall buttes as he forded the river, striking out for the further bank. The sky still held the last vestiges of daylight, sufficiently for him to be able to make out details clearly around him. Snorting a little, the sorrel clambered stiff-legged up the smooth shingly bank, moved for a couple of feet along the trail, then stopped suddenly, shying away in sharp alarm.

Bending forward, Dave controlled his mount, peering off into the gloom beneath the trees. At first, he could see nothing to account for the animal's behaviour. Then he saw the lone tree, standing some distance apart from the others in the middle of a small clearing to one side of the trail. One of the lowermost branches, as thick as a man's body, thrust itself out at right angles from the trunk so that it grew virtually horizontally, away from the trail. Slipping from the saddle, he advanced a couple of feet into the clearing and paused to stare, his left hand hovering just above the Colt in its holster. He experienced a sudden tightening of the muscles of his jaw at what he saw there. The three bodies dangling from the ropes, side by side, had evidently been left there as a kind of warning, an act of the type of rough justice meted out in the hard country along the frontier of the west.

Going closer, he saw that all three men had been shot before they had been hanged. Evidently, whoever had done this had decided that shooting was not good enough for these men. For a moment, standing there, considering the scene in front of him, he wondered just who these men might be, and what their crime had been which had necessitated them dying in this brutal manner. All three looked like ordinary cowpokes. There was nothing about them which suggested they were killers or crooked gamblers.

Going back to the trembling horse, he swung himself up into the saddle and rode on more cautiously now, every sense more alert after what he had seen. Absently, his left hand eased the gun in its holster, moving it gently up and down, fingers curled around the butt as if they belonged there and nowhere else. He could not explain to himself why he felt so apprehensive at what he had seen. Those men could have been dead for days, there was little way of telling. The men who had been responsible would not stick around the place of execution once they had finished their work.

He dipped down low into the undulating hills, splashed his horse across a small, pebbly stream, climbed another grade. His original intention of making camp on the bank of the Smoky had been forgotten in the sight of the dead men back there. He decided to ride on for another hour before stopping for the night, knowing that he would not make it now into Fenton before the next day.

Ahead of him, the land began to break once more into a jumbled mass of rocks and sharp-backed ridges through which the trail, narrowed at that point, seemed to be the only comfortable passage for a man on horseback. Tremaine frowned as he rode towards it. He guessed that the roughness would pass for perhaps a mile or so before it broadened out again into greener, flatter country. Sitting straight in the saddle, he listened to the various night sounds all around him and assessed them carefully, eyes narrowed down. There was the crackling rustle of the breeze in the thorn cactus which dotted the rocks and the faint, grating whine of the innumerable grains of sand where they abraded the sandstone.

He heard nothing unusual, but the stillness that lay clamped tightly down against the boulders and ridges, was something he did not like. Try as he would, he could not get the image of those three dead men out of his mind. There was something big brewing in this part of the territory if men had to die like that.

The sharp crack of the rifle came as a distinct surprise to him. The sorrel kicked itself forward instinctively and the slug struck the rocky wall immediately behind him, whining off in murderous ricochet. A second bullet struck the saddlehorn, glanced off the tough leather, striking so close that he felt the breath of it pass his cheek.

Savagely, he kicked spurs into the horse's flanks, sent it racing for the cover of a cluster of tall rocks that bordered the trail a score or so yards away. As he rode, he bent his head low over the sorrel's neck, jerked the Colt from its holster. He had spotted the spurting flashes from the rifle as the hidden marksman had fired down at him from his vantage point among the rocks. He knew almost exactly where the other was. Sliding swiftly from the saddle, he moved into the long dark shadows that lay among the boulders, crouching low, his feet making scarcely any sound on the hard shale. He knew that he had to move fast and silently and stay behind the protective bulkiness of the rocks until he got within sight of the other. As he worked his way up, he strained his ears to pick out the sounds of a man moving deeper into the rocks, but there was nothing. Clearly the other was unsure whether or not he had been hit, was not going to attempt to move and give away his position until he was sure.

Working his way around a rocky outcrop, he bore to the left, making a circuit of the spot where he reckoned the drygulcher to be. Pausing in the deep shadow of the rock, he peered about him. From somewhere close at hand came the faint whinney of a horse. Grinning a little in the darkness, he moved forward, bent low, the Colt held tightly in his left hand, finger bar-straight on the trigger. He had not fired a shot yet, knew that he had to get within sighting distance of the other before he gave away his position. Sliding forward, he edged between a sharp-sided cleft in the rocks. There was plenty of cover here fortunately and the whinney of the other's mount had given him a lead.

He caught sight of the animal a few moments later. It stood hobbled near a stunted tree, the reins looped around a broken branch. There he stopped and listened carefully, waiting for the hidden killer to give away his position. The silence grew, lengthened. Sooner or later the other would break, would make a move, either towards the overhang so that he could look down on to the trail, or back in the direction of his mount, so that he might saddle up and ride on out of there. Either way, Tremaine felt sure he would be able to pick out the other before the bush-whacker knew where he was.

Since both shots had been fired from the same rifle, he judged there was only one man here, otherwise they would have placed themselves on either side of the canyon, hoping to catch him in a murderous crossfire. Two minutes passed, the seconds ticking themselves away into a dark eternity. Then he caught the faint scrape of a boot against rock as the hidden dry-gulcher moved. Dave started forward again, gliding from one rock to another, keeping his head low so that at no time was he outlined on the skyline.

Another soft sound, carrying well in the still night air. He turned his head very slowly. The dry-gulcher was moving deeper into the rocks now, easing his way back from the trail. Dave made up his mind to forestall this move and wriggled down a narrow gully, through a cactus thicket and out on to a broad ledge where he could see for several yards in both directions. Moments later he caught a glimpse of the dark shadow, moving slowly and cautiously less than ten yards away. The rifleman was crouched down behind a line of boulders and even from that distance, Tremaine could see the other's nervous movements, guessed that the other had lost him, had already decided that the man he had attempted to kill might be stalking him through the rocks.

Reaching around with his right hand he picked up a small stone, judged the distance and tossed it a little to the other's left. The rattle as it struck the rocks was clearly audible in the taut stillness. The shadow moved, swinging round, the rifle barrel tilting upwards.

Swiftly Dave rose to his feet, moved out into the open, standing close to the huge boulder which had hidden him from the other.

'Hold it right there,' he snapped harshly.

The other stiffened, stood quite still. Then, as if realizing that any further attempt at resistance could lead only to a quick demise, dropped the rifle with a clatter on to the hard ground.

'Now you're showin' sense.' Still watchful, ready for any

move, Dave stepped forward, coming up to the other.
'Now turn around so I can have a good look at you.'

For a second, the other remained perfectly still and
Tremaine, seized with a sudden anger, grabbed the other's
shoulder, jerked sharply. The first suspicion came as he
felt the softness of the flesh beneath his fingers. Then the
broadbrimmed sombrero tilted a little as the other was
whirled sharply around and he saw the moonlight gleam
faintly on the long, chestnut hair, saw the round, pale
features that stared up at him. She was tall for a woman,
which explained why he had thought it was a man standing there. She wore a dark blue shirt and he saw that
although she was on guard against him, there was no look
of fear in her face.

'Well,' she said harshly, 'why don't you use that gun? Is
it that you're afraid of what might happen to you when
you get back to town? It can't be that you're against shooting women.'

Baffled, Dave stared down at her, then thrust the Colt
back into its holster. He felt unsure of himself. 'Why did
you try to kill me back there?' he asked tightly, in an
attempt to cover up his confusion. 'This seems one hell of
a welcome for a stranger ridin' in.'

For the first time, a look of uncertainty crossed the
girl's face. 'I didn't shoot to kill,' she said flatly. 'If I had,
you'd have been dead by now. You made a perfect target
down there.'

'Then why?'

The brown-haired girl looked at him steadily. 'You're
with that outfit who have been trying to run us off our
land.' He saw the anger that blazed momentarily in her
eyes.

'So I'm ridin' with some outfit. Why would I be doin'
that? You ain't never set eyes on me before, have you?'

'No, but that doesn't mean that—'

Dave said gently. 'I'm ridin' with nobody, lady. I've been
on the trail for more days than I care to remember. I'm
headin' into Fenton on business. When I've finished that,

I'll be on my way back again. Believe me, if there's some range war startin' here I want no part in it.'

The girl bit her lower lip, rubbed her shoulder a little where his fingers must have bitten into the flesh. 'Then you're not one of Jed Sabine's men?'

Tremalne shook his head. 'Never heard of the man,' he asserted. 'Was he responsible for those men back there near the river? I came across three of them hanging from a tree branch there.'

The girl started and her eyes narrowed on him in appraisal. 'Where was this?' she asked quickly. She glanced swiftly around them as if wondering if they were alone.

'Just this side of the Smoky,' he answered. 'I figured there might be trouble brewin' in these parts when I came on 'em. They'd been shot as well as hanged.'

She was listening to his voice, weighing what he said, evidently deep in thought. She had started out being suspicious of him and he had the feeling that in spite of what he had said, she wanted to stay that way, but was not finding it easy to do so. Still, he saw the change in the set of her lips, saw the rapid gust of expression that went over her regular features. 'So that's what happened to them.' Her voice was little more than a husky whisper. Her mouth was pressed tightly together and he heard the bitterness in her tone as she lifted her head and went on: 'We lost three men today. They were guarding part of our herd at the line camp on the edge of the spread. We thought that with all the trouble, they may have decided to ride on over the hill without bothering to come in for their wages first. Evidently we were wrong. It must have been Sabine's men who killed them and hung them there as a warning to anyone else.'

Dave remained silent, watching her struggle with her feelings, waiting for her to go on, knowing that, if she trusted him, she might want to explain things to him. Evidently there was big trouble here and Clem had not been exaggerating when he had asked him to come.

At length, she stirred herself as if she had just become

aware of his presence there. Tiredly, she said: 'What are you going to do now?'

He shrugged. 'I'd figured on makin' camp on the banks of the Smoky for the night. What I found there kind of put that thought out of my mind. I was ridin' on a little way when your first bullet just missed me.'

'Saddle up and ride back to the ranch with me. After what I did back there, I guess the only thing I can do to really apologize is see that you get a decent bed for the night.'

'What ranch?' he asked.

'The Double C. Not one of the biggest spreads in the territory, but I'm sure my father will be only too pleased to put you up for the night.' When she noticed him hesitate at her offer, she went on quickly: 'Besides, my father will want to know what you found on the trail here. Those men deserve decent burial.'

As if taking his continued silence for acceptance, she turned and walked along the narrow gully to where her horse was tethered, picking up her Winchester on the way. When she came back, leading the horse by the reins, the rifle in the scabbard beside the saddle, she said: 'You sure that horse of yours will still be around?'

Dave nodded. He led the way down the treacherous slope. The night was still silent all about them as they rode out the deep canyon, heading north-west. By now, it was completely dark with only the moonlight and starshine to provide any light. The girl sat square in her saddle, scarcely looking at him as the trail looped between tall stands of red-barked pine through which the moon glinted brilliantly.

'What sort of business is it you have in Fenton, Mister—'

'Dave Tremaine,' he said with a faint smile, his teeth showing white in the shadowed face. 'As for my business, I'm trying to locate an old partner of mine – man by the name of Clem Fordyce.'

She gave him a keen glance, then looked away swiftly.

'Fordyce?' she said, her tone clearly a little sharper than she had intended.

'That's right. You know him?'

'No. I've never heard that name before. But if he's a townsman, it isn't surprising. We have very little to do with the townsfolk.'

Inwardly, he had the feeling that she was not telling him the truth. It had been evident that she had heard Clem's name before; yet if that was so, why had she denied it like this? Did she still not trust him? Was she perhaps afraid of him and his reasons for being there?

'You sound as though you don't like the townsfolk?'

'Like them?' There was vehemence in her tone, but she forced it away with an effort. 'Some of them may be all right, I suppose. But most of them are nothing more than crooked gamblers and hired killers. The railroad pushed the rails as far as Fenton and then built a railhead here. I guess you know what that means. Every tinhorn gambler and footpad, every saloon operator and cheap dance hall girl came flocking into Fenton, especially when the gold was found in the El Dorado hills to the north. It's a hell town now. They come to buy up land and speculate with it, making fortunes at the expense of the decent people who come here looking for a home, a place to put down their roots and build something really worthwhile out of the country.'

'Surely they have law and order in Fenton?'

'Law and order,' the girl snorted derisively. 'Haven't you even seen a hell-town once the speculators and big men move in, mister?'

Dave nodded his head slowly. 'I've seen 'em,' he said softly. He did not mention that he had helped to clean up two or three of them in his career. That part of his life was perhaps best not mentioned until he knew where he stood and just what the score was in this neck of the territory. Tightening his lips, he rode in reflective silence beside the girl as they moved over a long meadow.

There had once been a town called Yellow Forks; a

small community until the railroad had come, the steel rails driving through the town, splitting it into two groups. The decent folk stayed on one side of the tracks, the gamblers and riffraff on the other. Yellow Forks had been a powder keg then with a damnably short fuse, burning fast. He had ridden in just as the whole lot had exploded and it had seemed for a time that the killer element would win out and take over control of the town. A lot of blood had been shed before they had finally been defeated. Maybe the same thing was about to happen to Fenton; maybe this time, without a quick gun, the lawless breed would succeed in taking over, in electing their own crooked lawmen, hiding behind a tin star and dispensing their own brand of justice.

Like the kind of justice which had clearly been meted out to those three riders whose bodies he had found on the banks of the Smoky river. It did not take much along the frontier to turn a stretch of territory into a jungle, harbouring men with the minds of jungle animals, stray and vicious, pale-eyed killers ready to sell their gun to the highest bidder, finish the job and move on to other pastures.

As they rode down a smooth moonlit slope, the girl said quietly: 'I don't suppose you would be looking for a job? Since we lost those three men, we're short-handed on the ranch and whatever you are, you look like a man used to the saddle, and maybe to cattle.'

Dave smiled. 'I'll admit that I've spent some time herdin' cattle, but I'm not lookin' for a job. Like I said, I've got business in town and when that's finished, I aim to ride on. I want no part of a range war. I've seen what can happen too often in the past, especially to anybody who rides into the middle of it.'

The girl did not make any further comment, but set her face to the front. Out of the corner of his eye, Dave could see that she was both displeased and contemptuous. He could tell from the set of her mouth and jaw what she was thinking. That he was a trail-drifter, maybe a dangerous one at that, looking for vengeance, just one more rider with perhaps a dishonourable past, keeping one jump ahead of the law. The judgement bothered him a little, but he put the thought out of his mind. He had more to worry him than that. The way things were shaping up, his task was not going to be an easy one.

Half an hour later they rode down a draw, came out around the wide curve of a hill and he noticed the ranch-house directly beneath them. A few lights showed in the windows that overlooked the wide courtyard and as they rode over a narrow plank bridge which spanned the small stream at the base of the hill and moved into the court-yard, the porch door opened and a man appeared there, silhouetted briefly against the light before he stepped quickly to one side, into the deep shadows on the veranda.

As he rode beside the girl into the courtyard, Dave noticed other men near the barn and bunkhouse, watch-ful men, he saw, alert for trouble. The idea sent a little chill through him, tightened the muscles of his chest. The swift, instinctively-made movement of the man on the porch had spoken more than mere words. It had been the action of a man afraid to show himself against the light for more than a few seconds, for fear of attracting a bullet out of the surrounding darkness.

'It's me, father,' called the girl loudly. She rode up to the porch and dismounted. 'I picked this man up on the trail a few miles back. I think he can tell us what happened to Charlie and the others.'

The man on the veranda lifted a hand, made a quick gesture with it. 'You're welcome, stranger. Ben will put your horse into the corral and see he's fed. You can get yourself a bed in the bunkhouse when you've had coffee and somethin' to eat.'

Dave got down from the saddle, handed his mount over to the man who stepped forward out of the shadows, then followed the girl into the house. He noticed that she continued to watch him, eyeing him closely now that she

was able to see him clearly for the first time. There was
little change in her expression and it was impossible to tell
what she was thinking at that moment.

'Take a seat at the table,' said the tall, grey-haired man,
waving towards a chair. 'My name is Lex Corrie. Since my
daughter has vouched for you, you're welcome.' He
glanced at the girl as she closed the parlour door. 'Where
did you say you found him, Virginia?'

'The far edge of the flats, father. I thought he was one
of Sabine's men. I'm afraid I took a couple of shots at
him.'

'Fortunately for me, her aim wasn't too good,' Dave
said, with a faint smile.

Corrie gave him a curious glance. He said slowly: 'She
wouldn't have missed, my friend, if she'd had a mind to hit
you.'

There was a faint smile in Dave's eyes, but he made no
comment beyond giving the girl an appraising glance.

Corrie said: 'You know somethin' about those three
hands of mine?'

'If they are the same men I came across just after
fordin' the Smoky, then they're hanging from the branch
of one of the trees there.'

Corrie gave Dave a bright-sharp glance. His eyes were
very still and in their depths a great anger formed and
moved slowly. 'This is more of Sabine's work. He threatened to destroy all of the smaller ranchers and this is his
way of goin' about it.'

'If that's what he's set on doin', then why don't you all
band together and fight? If you sit back and do nothin',
then he'll pick you off one by one.'

Virginia Corrie came into the room from the small
kitchen. She carried a tray and a pot of coffee, setting
them down on the table in front of Dave. He poured milk
from the tin of condensed milk and spooned sugar out of
the bowl. She was watching him closely all of the time, still
a trifle uncertain of him, suspicious of a stranger, puzzled
about his intentions there and the unsureness gave soft

contours to her face, heightening the red curve of her lips where they lay close together.

Corrie said harshly, leaning back in his chair. 'There are ways here on the frontier which you possibly don't comprehend. Evil ways. Sabine came here four years ago just when the railroad started pushing the rails west towards Fenton. He built up his stock and bought up all of the available land at rock bottom prices. Some he sold out to the railroad for more'n three hundred per cent profit. But for all that he sold, he got as much in return by driving the homesteaders and smaller ranchers off their property. He holds mortgages on most of the ranches in the surrounding territory and he brought in a bunch of hired gunslicks to back up any move he made. You can't expect men to go up against an outfit like that, even if you tell 'em that there's every chance of winnin' through in the end.'

'So you're doin' nothin'.' Dave sipped the scalding hot coffee. It burned his tongue and throat, but brought some of the life and warmth back into his body. The girl came back a few minutes later with potatoes and beans and jerked beef and he ate ravenously.

'You wouldn't be lookin' for a job, would you?' Corrie asked, as he pushed the cleaned plate away, drained the second cup of coffee and sat back, bringing out the makings of a smoke, rolling the tobacco gently in the brown paper.

The other watched him as he asked the question and when Dave only shook his head slightly and smiled at the almost pleading expression on the man's face, the other's expression darkened a little, then he shrugged as if it was the answer he had expected.

'I guess you're like all of the crowd that comes ridin' through these parts.' he said. 'You never stay anywhere in one place long. Most of the fly-by-nights who come this way are just ahead of the law.'

'And you think I'm one of those men?'

'I hope not. If I was to find that you'd gone over to

Sabine after my offer of a job here I'd see that you didn't
live to double-cross another honest man. But you don't
have the look of the lawless about you, in spite of the look
of that gun you're wearin'.' He inclined his head towards
the smooth butt of the Colt. 'I go on a first, quick judgement of a man. But there have been times in the past
when I've been proved wrong and now I'm not so sure of
that judgment as far as any man is concerned.'

From the tone of the other's words, Dave guessed that
there was something in the other's past about which he
did not want to talk, did not even want to be reminded. He
decided not to push the questions.

Getting to his feet, he said: 'Reckon I'll turn in, Corrie.
I've been ridin' that trail for days now. First time I'll have
slept on a real bed in all that time.'

Corrie stirred himself from his deep, reflective thought,
nodded. 'Virginia will show you the bunkhouse,' he said
quietly. 'We can maybe talk again in the morning.'

As they walked across the quiet, shadowed courtyard in
the direction of the bunkhouse, Dave asked: 'What's your
father afraid of, Virginia?'

She looked at him sharply, uttered a tight little laugh
that had no mirth in it. 'You're very perceptive,' she said
after a pause.

'When you ride the trail alone, you have to be.'

Virginia's look seemed cool and distant as she said
softly: 'Not that it's really any business of yours, but it's the
memory of my brother that still rankles with him,
although he never mentions him now.'

'Your brother's dead then?' Dave said in a low tone. He
halted in the middle of the courtyard.

She shook her head. 'Not dead as you know death, but
he might as well be as far as we are concerned.'

'I'm afraid I don't understand.' He looked down at her
upturned face, puzzled.

'He left the ranch more than a year ago, rode into
Fenton, said there were more opportunities of making
money there than here on the land acting as nursemaid to

a bunch of cattle. I think he lost a lot of money to some crooked gambler. That's how he fell in with Sabine.'

'He's workin' for Sabine?'

'Yes.'

Standing there, Dave saw her feelings come to her face and lips; saw the way her eyes narrowed and lose their warmth. It was as if something had just gone out of her. She said: 'Since then, his name has never been mentioned by my father. He treats him as if he's dead. But somehow, sometimes . . . I think that he remembers and wishes he were back.'

TWO

GUNSLICK

At eleven o'clock the next morning, three men rode the dusty trail that led into Fenton. The sun was high, climbing swift to the zenith and already the heat head was approaching it's limit of piled-up intensity. They rode with the brims of their hats pulled well down over their faces, angled across the square, reined up in front of the Broken Lance saloon and went inside.

One was a man of middle-age, greying at the temples, his face dark and swarthy and bearded. The other two were younger men, one little more than a youth, with a shock of fiery red hair and pale grey eyes, the other five or six years older, stockily-built, blue eyes screwed up a little to counteract the vicious glare of the sun. The older man, Jeff Forrest, was foreman of the Circle Diamond ranch, owned by Jed Sabine, the others were Shorty Frye and Luke Corrie.

Inside the saloon, Forrest paused and looked about him. It was still a little early in the day for much business and customers were few, nevertheless there were four men playing faro at one of the circular tables and as Forrest let his gaze traverse the room he saw Sabine seated alone at the table furthest from the door.

Walking over to the other, Forrest stood in front of the
table, staring silently down at his boss. Where he would
have resented the foreman's manner in other men,
Sabine tended to overlook his lack of manners. He
knew that he had a good and loyal man here, one who
would carry out orders and ask no questions. Forrest
had been instrumental in building him up into what he
now was – the most powerful man in and around
Fenton.

Signalling to the bartender with a quick, imperious jerk
of his right hand, Sabine motioned to the empty chair
opposite him. 'You look like a man with a load of trouble
on his shoulders,' he said harshly.

Forrest nodded his head in affirmation. 'Might be at
that.' He poured a long drink from the bottle which the
bartender set in front of him, tossed it over in a couple
of quick gulps, and poured a second, standing the glass
in front of him and staring down at it as he said:
'Stranger rode in to the territory last night. Seems he
met up with Virginia Corrie, spent the night at their
place.'

'You think perhaps they sent for him – some hired
gun from the border?' Sabine asked with a note of
interest in his tone. The news did not particularly worry
him. The smaller ranchers were for ever bringing in
men who considered themselves fast with a gun. Their
reputation never seemed to hold up when it came to a
decision. Either they forked their broncs and faded out
over the hills when they learned the full extent of the
opposition, or they made their play against one of his
men and ended up in Boot Hill, six feet under the clay.
Either way, they caused him little trouble. Indeed, at
times it amused him to see the way in which the ranchers acted once their hired guns were no longer there to
afford them any feeling of protection. Very often, it had
turned out to be the best thing that could have
happened, for it prompted the ranchers to sell out to
him now that they found themselves naked and

defenceless, knowing that he could ride in and smash them utterly.

Forrest rubbed a hand down the side of his face, forehead furrowed in thought. 'Could be that, I reckon. But Frye yonder—' He jerked a thumb towards the bar, where Frye and Luke Corrie were drinking together, '—overheard some conversation last night after this *hombre* had ridden in. Seems he's got some kind of business here in town. He was offered a job by Corrie's father, but turned it down.'

He paused for comment from the other and when it did not appear to be forthcoming, went on hastily: 'He gave his name as Dave Tremaine.'

'You ever heard of a *hombre* by that name?' asked Sabine weightily.

The foreman took time over his reply. After several moments consideration, he said: 'The name sounds familiar from way back. Not around these parts, I'm sure of that. I'd say he's just another of those hellions from near the border, quick with a gun, anxious to prove his reputation and then move on once he gets his pay. We've seen 'em come before – and we've watched 'em go, one way or the other.'

'That's as may be,' grunted Sabine. He lit a thin black cheroot, blew the smoke out in twin streams through his nostrils. 'But he could still mean trouble for us and right now, that's somethin' I don't want. If he ever gets the edge on us, he could even get these ranchers to band together to fight me and the first thing you know, we'll have a full scale range war on our hands.' He shrugged and spread his hands a little. 'I've no doubt whatever as to the outcome of such a fight, but it will mean I'll lose a lot of my best men just at a time when I'm aimin' to consolidate my position here. There's one hell of a lot at stake right now, too much for me to throw away by takin' stupid and unnecessary chances with one man.'

'You want him to be got rid of before he can make any

trouble?' The foreman spoke in a matter-of-fact manner as if he were simply discussing the ordinary everyday work on the ranch.

Sabine nodded shortly. 'That's exactly what I do want, Forrest. You see this *hombre* yourself?'

The foreman shook his head, drained the whisky from the glass, wiped the back of his hands over his laps. 'All this I heard from Frye. He works for Corrie, rode into the line camp at sunup this morning with the news. I figgered you ought to know about it right away.'

Sabine nodded. 'All right, then you handle it as you see fit. You're sure you know how to go about stoppin' this *hombre*? If he's fast with a gun, he could be hard to handle.'

Forrest grinned viciously. 'I was figgerin' on havin' Cantry fix him,' he said with relish. 'Tremaine will be ridin' into town some time today. He'll start noseyin' around, askin' questions. Don't worry, when he does that, Cantry will fix him.'

Sabine pondered that for a moment, then nodded agreement. 'Find Cantry and tell him I agree. I want Tremaine dead before sundown. You got that?'

'I'll see to it,' said Forrest incisively. Scraping back his chair, he pushed himself to his feet. Going over to the bar, he ordered another drink, stood there in deep conversation with the other two men for several minutes before departing.

From the table in the corner, Sabine watched him leave, then flicked his glance back to Frye and Corrie. How far he could trust either of these men, he was uncertain. Frye would turn and run at the first sign of tough gunplay. His only advantage lay in the fact that he worked for Corrie and was therefore a spy in the enemy's camp, could feed back information as to what Corrie's intentions were almost as soon as the old fool knew them himself. Even now, Sabine felt sure that if he could just fix Corrie once and for all, he would have virtually won the battle for control of the land around Fenton. It was only because in the other's stubbornness the rest of the ranchers thought they saw a champion for their cause, that they were holding out as long as this. He had figured that once the news of what had happened to Corrie's three trail hands leaked out, it would have convinced everybody concerned that Corrie was finished. Now this *hombre* Tremaine had turned up from nowhere and put a spoke into the wheel.

Crushing out the butt of his cheroot, he stared fixedly into space, trying to adjust his plans in the face of this fresh information. He was not unduly troubled. Tremaine, even if he did throw in his lot with Corrie, was only one man, would stand no chance of tipping the scales against him, even if he tried. But there was no doubt in his mind, that the sooner Tremaine was dead or run out of town, the better.

He moistened his lips, then motioned the two men at the bar to come over to him. They stood in front of him a trifle uncertainly. Corrie flashed him a quick, significant look, but said nothing.

'This *hombre* who rode in last night, Luke. You ever see him before? One of your father's friends, maybe?'

'You know I haven't seen my father for almost a year. I know very little of his friends.'

Sabine pursed his lips into a thin, tight line. For a moment it seemed some harsh, angry retort was on his lips, then he sat forward, resting his elbows on the table, leaning his weight on them, the tips of his fingers placed gently together.

He let his glance slide towards Frye. 'You say you saw this man and heard somethin' of what they were talkin' about?'

Frye nodded. 'I ain't never seen him before.'

'But you know why he's here?'

Frye hesitated, glanced obliquely at Corrie. 'There was some talk, but I figure we'd better discuss it alone.'

'If it concerns my father, you can say whatever you have in your mind in front of me,' Luke Corrie said harshly. 'You know damned well that I—'

Sabine stopped him with a lift of his hand. 'Better go get yourself another drink, Luke,' he said quietly.

Corrie shot Frye a venomous glance, brows drawn down tight over his eyes. Then he muttered an oath under his breath and moved off in the direction of the bar, knocking over a couple of chairs on the way.

Frye waited until the other was out of earshot, then leaned forward a little and lowering his voice said: 'There was talk about that prospector, Clem Fordyce. Seems he was a friend of Tremaine's.'

Sabine sucked in a sharp gust of wind. 'So that's it.' He stared at the other closely. 'You're sure of this?'

'Damned sure,' affirmed the other. 'It may be that when he starts askin' questions around Fenton, he'll get answers he doesn't like. Way I hear it, Virginia Corrie is still mighty fond of her brother in spite of what happened a year ago. She sure won't like the *hombre* who picks a fight and shoots him down.'

Sabine smiled, but there was no mirth in the faint twitching of his lips and it never reached his eyes. 'I've been worried about Luke for some time now. The only hold I've got over him is that money he owes.' He nodded his head very slowly. 'Now I've got somethin' else. If he was to step out of line, I could always threaten to turn him over to Tremaine as the man who shot Fordyce in the back.'

At high noon, Fenton lay slumbering in the hollow among the hills. The bowl acted as a natural heat and dust trap and as Tremaine reined up his mount on the brow of the low hill overlooking the town, he could see the dust devils chasing themselves slowly along the wide main street and the heat shimmering the roofs of the buildings that lay on either side of the main street, with the narrower alleys running back from it to the outskirts of the town. There was a substantial wooden bridge across the river at the bottom of the slope, replacing the precarious planking bridge which he remembered from his last visit to Fenton and it was evident that a great many changes had been wrought in the town during the time he had been away. There were scarcely any gaps left between the houses, a host of new stores had been put up and around the wide square, he could make out a bank and two saloons which had not been there when he had known the town.

Certainly Clem had not exaggerated when he had said that the town had grown during the past few years. Over to his right, curving in over the vast stretch of the valley, out to the pass between the rising stone columns of the mountains, were the gleaming metal rails of the railroad which had been pushed this far west and now terminated at the railhead on the edge of town. From where he sat, he could just make out the stockpens alongside the loading point, a few full of milling cattle waiting to be put on board the train that stood at the terminal. A column of black smoke lifted high into the still air from the tall funnel of the locomotive and the faint hissing of steam reached his ears.

Leaning forward over the saddlehorn, he took out the tobacco pouch and made himself a smoke. The heat of the sun was a tremendous burning pressure on everything around him, burning through the cloth of his jacket into his back and shoulders and he was forced to narrow his eyes against the punishing glare that lifted from all about him, reflected from the rocks and sand, from the glittering river and the windows of the buildings in town. The tobacco smoke burned his mouth and throat and brought little refreshment, but there were times when a cigarette could be used for other purposes than enjoyment. It relaxed him yet seemed to sharpen his senses so that he appeared to be aware of all that was going on in the town which lay spread out below him. He could make out virtually every section of Fenton, could see a buckboard swinging slowly along the main street. The stage stood outside the depot, the horses standing patiently in the traces. He doubted if they would be moving out during the full heat of the day. In front of one of the saloons, he could see a swamper pushing his brush along the slatted boardwalk, sweeping the rubbish to the corner and then out into the street.

There was what looked like a school house on the far edge of town, within a stone's throw of the church that lifted its white steeple above the buildings in its vicinity. Flicking his half-finished cigarette on to the ground, he touched spurs to the sorrel's flanks, urged it down the slope. A few minutes later he was clumping across the wide bridge, the hollow echoes ringing in his ears. As he rode into the main street, he cast about him with curious eyes, trying to pick out the few landmarks he recalled from his last visit to the town.

At first sight, everything seemed so changed that it was as if he were riding into a trail town he had never seen before. But after a few moments, while his mind fought to orientate itself, he made out the tiny store now crushed between a large livery stable and a brand-new hotel. There were many more saloons and gambling houses here than he remembered and here and there, along the narrow streets which opened off the main road running straight through the town, he could see other buildings which were still under construction.

Inwardly, he debated whether this was a good thing as far as Fenton was concerned. He did not doubt that at some time in the future, once the town had outgrown its growing pains it would prove to be of general good for the place; but right now, with the lawless elements moving in on the place, anxious to fill their own pockets with gold, to seize power wherever possible, and not caring overmuch how they did it, or who died in the process, it was not a safe or pleasant place in which a decent citizen might live. He had seen

nearly a dozen similar trail towns up and down the
frontier and in every case, the old ways of violence and
death, never changing, never in any way different,
always worked their way through these towns, isolating
them and their history into a small stretch of time.
Maybe it was a law of nature that every town worth its
salt had to go through this bloody section of its history
before it could grow up into something really big and
worthwhile.

At this hour of high noon there were not many citizens
in sight. A few lounged in high-backed chairs, seeking the
shade provided by the wide overhangs along the boardwalks and there were several horses tethered at the hitch-
ing rails outside the saloons, testifying to the fact that
there was a thirsty populaion in the town of Fenton.
Maybe later in the day, when the sun dropped towards the
high mountains to the north and west, and a cooling
breeze blew through the streets, there would be more
activity, more people stirring.

A tall, hatchet-faced man lounged against the door of
the Sheriff's Office. Dave noticed him when he was still
some distance away, saw the man eye him with a frankly
curious gaze, then suddenly twist the handle of the office
door and step inside, closing the door behind him. As
Tremaine drew level with the building, one of the
curtains over the dusty windows was twitched aside and
he caught a fragmentary glimpse of two faces peering
out, watching his steady progress towards the middle of
town.

Diagonally across the square from the two-storey hotel,
was a small livery stable. It was a low-roofed, one-storey
affair, the interior dark. He rode over to it, swung from the
saddle and led the sorrel forward. A man drifted out of the
dim interior, a straw in has mouth. He eyed Tremaine with
a flat, incurious stare, as if he was accustomed to leave any
curiosity concerning strangers to others.

'Howdy,' he said, speaking around the straw. 'Just
ridden in?'

Dave gave him a quick nod. He handed the reins to the groom. 'Feed him and see he gets the best of everythin',' he said.

'You goin' to be in town long?' inquired the other. His glance slanted up at Dave from beneath the tilted brim of his greasy hat.

'Depends. Two, three days – maybe. I'm lookin' for information.'

The other's eyes narrowed fractionally. There was a faint look of bright, beady wisdom in them. Dave knew that in a town such as this, the groom at the livery stable, in common with the blacksmith, was the man who saw most of what went on, knew most of the rumours and could generally sift the truth from the fiction. Whether the other would talk or not, was something he did not know ; and there was the big question of whether he could be trusted.

'I guess I see a lot of what goes on, and I hear more,' said the other with a sly glance. He turned and led the sorrel into the rear of the stables, placed it into one of the stalls and pulled off the saddle, placing it on the post alongside the stall. Taking out a plug of tobacco, he bit off a wad with a sharp twist of his teeth, began to chew it slowly and methodically. 'Trouble is that if I started to talk about what I know, I wouldn't be alive long. Too many eyes watchin' and ears listenin' in this town. Everybody walkin' around softly just waitin' for some-thin' to happen and blow the whole place skyhigh. It's a real hell of a town.'

He spat a stream of brown juice into the straw in one corner. His flesh was burned a deep, brick-red by long exposure to the strong sunlight and his eyebrows were bleached so white that at first it seemed they were non-existent. The eyes were of a pale watery blue and the mouth was weak, with a prominent underlip.

'I've learned somethin' of the way the place has grown since I rode through here some years ago.' Dave leaned his back against one of the wooden uprights, watched the other closely.

'Sure is changin',' agreed the groom. 'Not for the better either.'

'So I figured,' mused Dave thoughtfully. 'I suppose it all started when they found gold in the hills to the north?'

'That's right. We got every kind of man here when that happened. Even when the major veins were finished, they still kept comin'. Those goddamn hills are nearly a hundred miles long and thirty miles deep. Nobody could cover all that for sure, so I guess anybody who did come in late reckoned that the big vein hadn't been found and they had as good a chance as anybody.'

'You know any of these prospectors?'

'Some.'

'You ever hear of a man called Clem Fordyce?'

The groom's head came up sharply. His eyes were veiled now. He was silent for a long time, then he said harshly: 'Like I said, I'm still alive because I don't tell of things I know. Too many dead men around Fenton because they couldn't keep still tongues in their heads.'

'You afraid of somebody – Sabine perhaps?'

'Me? I'm afraid of everybody, so nobody bothers with me.' The other moved away from the stall, walking slowly back to the front of the stables. Pausing before they came within sight of anyone in the street, the other laid a hand on Dave's arm, said in a low, warning voice: 'Be careful who you talk to in town, and what you say. It ain't hard to get mixed in with the wrong crowd here.'

'You still know nothin' about Fordyce?'

The other shook his head. 'Very likely you could have a talk with Thompson. He's the undertaker in town. If anythin' happened to this friend of yours, then he'll be sure to know.'

'Then you know he's dead?' Dave turned, gave the other a sharp look.

'I don't know anythin',' persisted the other. 'But if you say he's around here and I don't know him, then I figure he's dead.'

This was obviously twisted reasoning on the other's part and Dave was sure the man knew far more than he was telling; but he also knew that nothing he could do or say would make the other talk. The man was scared and a frightened man would not talk freely unless he could be convinced that he would be afforded protection against the object of his fear. At the present time, Dave was not in any position to give this protection.

'Where can I find this *hombre*, Thompson?' he asked shortly.

The other raised an arm and pointed along the street. 'Just past the church,' he said, still chewing. 'You can't miss the funeral parlour.'

'Thanks.' Dave made his way across the square. He found the funeral parlour halfway along the street, standing in the shadow of the tall church tower. Standing on the boardwalk, he peered in through the thick glass of the window, trying to make out details in the gloomy interior, but he could see scarcely anything. So intent was he that he did not hear the man move into the doorway from inside the building and the first he knew of his presence was when the man said: 'Were you looking for something, mister?'

Dave jerked himself upright, feeling sheepish. The other was short, fat, and even though he had just stepped out of the apparently cool interior of the building and was in the shade of the doorway, he was perspiring visibly. He pulled out a red handkerchief and mopped his forehead.

'You'll be Thompson,' Dave said at length.

'That's right.' The man gave him an oily smile. 'What can I do for you?'

'A friend of mine had a gold workin' up there in the hills a little while ago. I figure he may have died. If so, then you'll be the only one in town who would bury him.'

There was a faint smirk on the undertaker's face. He mopped it again with the handkerchief. 'I'm the only undertaker in Fenton,' he said in answer to the question.

'Perhaps if you told me your friend's name, I can help you.'

'Clem Fordyce. The groom at the livery stables reckons he may be dead and buried by now and if he—' Dave broke off as he saw the sudden gust of expression that flashed across the other's features.

'You say you're a friend of his?'

'That's right.' Dave had the sure conviction now that there was something here which did not tie up. Something had happened as far as Clem was concerned, and whatever it was, no one in town wanted to talk to him about it. More and more, he got the feeling that it was something to do with Sabine. Had Clem been murdered for his claim, perhaps shot in the back by a dry-gulcher in some dark alley in town? Clem had been no mean hand with a gun in the old days, but undoubtedly the years would have slowed his fast draw now.

'Clem Fordyce was killed three weeks ago.' There was a slow finality in the man's tone. He spoke of death as if it were an everyday occurrence; an inevitable happening which did not touch him personally.

Dave felt the sudden sharp tightening of the muscles of his stomach at the news. It was something he had been expecting, a conviction that had grown stronger during those long days and nights on the trail; but it did something to hear it from this man. With an effort, he pulled himself together. His mouth and throat were dry and he ran the tip of his tongue around his lips.

'You know how it happened?'

The undertaker shook his head emphatically. 'A couple of men brought him here around midnight one night. They said they'd found him in an alley. He was dead when they got to him, but it looked as if there'd been some kind of gunplay because he had his gun in his hand, but it hadn't been fired.'

'But you must have examined the body. You can say if he was shot in the back or not?' Dave persisted.

The undertaker's eyes narrowed down, drawing the thick, black brows together. 'Just what are you gettin' at, mister?'

'Nothin'. Just tryin' to find out how he was killed. Seems to me that there are a lot of things goin' on in Fenton that I ought to know about. Nobody wants to talk about Clem, or how he died. My guess is that Sabine or some of his men are at the back of it, and they're all scared to talk.'

The other did not fall for the sarcasm in Dave's voice. He said very softly: 'You'd better walk real wide of Sabine, mister, if you want to stay healthy in Fenton. If you don't, then it sure could be that I'll be gettin' myself another customer before long.'

Dave smiled thinly. 'I don't aim to get myself killed, be sure of that. But I do mean to find out what happened to Clem Fordyce.'

The other turned, made as if to enter the shop, then paused and said: 'If you want my advice, mister, you'll fork your horse and ride on out of Fenton before there's trouble. You won't do any good rakin' over the past and what's best forgotten.'

Dave clenched his teeth. The other's manner seemed a trifle warmer than before, but he was still being enigmatical. He inferred some perverseness on the other's part, as if the man knew everything about this sordid business, but was determined to say nothing, maybe to force him to find out things for himself and run the risk of being shot in the process.

'If you won't tell me what happened, at least you can tell me where I can find Clem's grave.'

The undertaker hesitated, seemed to make up his mind on something. 'I didn't go along with the coffin,' he said finally. 'But you shouldn't have any difficulty findin' the spot. The graveyard is yonder, on the slope of the hill.' He pointed a hand along the narrow alley that wound up past the side of the church nearby.

As he made his way along the winding alley, Dave

thought things over in his mind. He did not quite know what to make of this. He had half-expected to find some reticence on the part of the townsfolk if Fordyce had been killed by some of Sabine's men so that the other might take over his claim, which he had inferred in his letter was a real bonanza. Knowing the greed of a man such as Sabine, he also knew that he would stand at nothing to get his hands on wealth such as that and it was becoming more and more obvious as time went on that Sabine was the real law in Fenton.

Above the level of the church, he pushed his way through a wooden gate that hung lop-sidedly on rusted hinges, clambered through an area of weeds which had overgrown most of the entrance. The rows of wooden crosses, many of them without inscription, testified to the wild and bloody beginnings which Fenton had had, a history of violence that was still, in some degree, going on yet. He found the fresh graves at one end of the graveyard, walked slowly along the row of crosses until he came to that which bore the name of Clem Fordyce. There was no other inscription and he stood for a long while, staring down at the final resting place of the man he had known almost the whole of his life. Although Clem had been older than him, there had existed a deep and lasting bond of friendship between these two men which could not be really broken, even now. Death had separated them, but the link remained.

He lifted his head and turned a little, staring sharply down at the town that lay stretched out beneath him, below his vantage point. Suddenly he hated the place. The depth of his intensity stirred him. He tried to reach far back with his thoughts to the old days, the carefree days, when there had been a deep sense of adventure with each new dawn and the trail that lay ahead of him was one filled with contentment and excitement; the smell of the cool mountain wind that came down from the high ridges when the world turned blue and still at evening, the orange glow of a campfire among tall, slender pines that

lifted to a sky glowing with a million pinpoints of light. He
tried to go back, further and further, but his mind found
nothing there that he could grasp and after a few
moments his body felt like a dried out husk, empty,
containing nothing. He had none of that sense of freedom
now. Very slowly, the realization came to him that after
today, he would never be able to return to the old times
and the old ways.

He rubbed his chin with the tips of his fingers. It was
a feeling he had never experienced before, something
akin to the awe he had felt when he had seen those
three bodies swinging from the branch of that tall tree
on the banks of the Smoky. The day would never dawn
again when he would be able to swing up lightly into
the saddle, ride out on to a fresh, new trail, filled with
the wonder of what he saw about him, and looked
forward to the night, not knowing where he would
build his campfire, never caring where darkness found
him. He felt a little shiver go through him, waited while
the brief spasm worked its way through his limbs. He
thought for a long moment of Fordyce, but the memory
brought a hurt to him that he could not thrust away and
his rage against this town was a searing flame inside
him.

He was so deeply absorbed in his thoughts that he did
not hear the man move up behind him. Not until the
other spoke was he aware of his presence.

'You'll be Dave Tremaine, I'm thinkin'.'

Slowly, Dave eased his hand away from the gun at his
waist. There was, he reasoned, no danger from the other.
The man was dressed in a black frock-coat, the tails flap-
ping a little around his knees. A shock of snow-white hair
was just visible beneath the wide-brimmed hat he wore and
his lined face bore a kindly look.

'I'm Doc Keller.' The other held out his hand and Dave
was momentarily surpised at the firmness of the old man's
grip. 'Hear you've been asking around in town about
Fordyce.'

Dave nodded, grinning bitterly. 'Nobody seems to want to talk about it. Seems to me there's some mystery attached to the way Clem died and I aim to find out what it is.'

'You're right when you say there's a mystery there, my friend,' agreed the other. 'As for the men who wouldn't talk, you can't really blame them. This town has seen far too much violence in the past few years. They can see no end to it, yet they won't band together to fight it and stamp out this evil once and for all.'

'Are you afraid to talk to me?' Dave asked.

The other smiled. 'I guess I have a somewhat privileged position in the town. The only doctor hereabouts, and Sabine knows that. Besides, I'm an old man and as a man gets older, he becomes less afraid to die.'

Dave drew in his breath slowly and just as slowly let it out again. 'You know who did it,' he said softly. He spoke in a mild tone as if this was something he would like to know but which did not stir him, not once betraying his emotions.

'I know who they say did it,' corrected the other quietly. He turned and led the way back through the tumble-down gate into the alley once more, walking slowly and stiffly in the bright, hot sunlight. 'That may not be the same thing.'

'You talk in riddles, Doctor,' Dave said. He had the uneasy feeling that the other was playing a cat-and-mouse game with him, just like the others, that when it came to the point, he would refuse point-blank to give him any information. He gave the other chance to speak, however, if he chose to speak, waiting hopefully as they walked on into the town.

'Clem Fordyce confided in me several times about that strike he made in the hills, mentioned you to me on many occasions. Seems you and he were great friends.'

Dave nodded at that as the other twisted his head round a little to peer curiously at him from beneath the black hat, but he made no comment, waited for Keller to go on.

'There are evil forces at work here in Fenton, as you probably already know. Men with the habits and thoughts of wolves; worse than animals in fact, for they kill for no reason than that they covet what another man has. There were several men who talked openly in the saloons of the gold that Fordyce had found. Some tried to trail him into the hills whenever he came into town for supplies, but he was too goddamn clever for 'em. They never found where he had made his strike. On the night it happened, Fordyce was in the Broken Lance saloon, drinking with a few of his cronies. There were plenty of Sabine's men there too, hoping to pick up some information no doubt that would give them a clue where his claim was.

'When he left, after drinking more than was really good for him, he headed for the rooming house where he put up whenever he was in town. Several of us saw him leave, though from what I heard later, nobody saw who, if any, of Sabine's men followed him.'

'But someone did follow him,' Dave said through tightly clenched teeth. 'Someone with a gun who shot him down in the darkness from ambush.'

Keller's eyes widened just a little as he looked sideways at Dave. Then he nodded his head. 'You're right, of course. Fordyce never had a chance. They said at the inquest that he was found with his gun in his hand, but that it hadn't been fired.' The doctor's smile was thin, a mere stretching of his lips. 'I examined the body as soon as I was called to it. He'd been shot in the back. He never knew what hit him and the gun was put in his hand after he was dead.'

Dave let his breath go softly through his teeth. 'That's the way I figured it,' he murmured. 'I knew that nobody would dare go up against him in even fight.' He thought of it slowly, his mind reaching forward and around the news, the truth of it coming into him in slow stages, hardening the lines of his face. His expression darkened.

'You know who did it?' he asked again, forming the words with a quiet deliberateness.

Keller nodded. 'It was Luke Corrie,' he said tightly. 'Virginia's brother.'

THREE

GUNPLAY

Tremaine stood wholly still as Keller told him. He felt
the coldness come to his face and a deep stillness settle
on his body. His eyes changed, narrowed and took on a
look which the old doctor had never seen before in the
eyes of any other man. Reaching out, Keller took the
other by the arm, said quietly: 'I think you'd better come
along with me. There are some things you ought to
know before you start jumpin' to the wrong conclu-
sions.'

'If Luke Corrie killed Clem, then I have no choice open
to me,' he said through stiff lips. 'I'd sooner it had been
any other man in town.' As he spoke, he remembered
Virginia Corrie as he had last seen her, standing on the
porch of the small ranch house, staring after him when he
had ridden off out of the yellow-sanded courtyard, heading for town. There had been some feeling in him at that
moment stronger than anything else he had ever known;
but now he felt it being washed away by the dark wave of
hatred that surged unbidden through him, swamping out
all other emotions.

'Yes,' said Keller. 'I know how you feel, son. But I still
think you should come with me, listen to what I have to
say.'

'Why?' Dave glanced at the other, momentarily puzzled.

'You came here with a chore to do. You thought that Fordyce was dead and you had to find out how it happened, who did it. How do you think this chore will leave you if you kill the wrong man?'

'That's strange talk,' Dave said harshly. 'Very strange talk indeed.'

'Perhaps, but you would do well to listen to it.' There was no denying the note of sincerity in the doctor's tone. He walked beside the other in silence as they moved across the square, along the wide main street. As they drew close to the Sheriff's office, the door opened and the hatchet-faced man that Dave had noticed when he had ridden into town, stepped out on to the board-walk.

He looked directly at Dave, said harshly: 'The name of Tremaine?'

Dave stopped, nodded. 'What's on your mind?' he asked. He caught the glint of sunlight on the deputy sheriff's badge the other wore on his vest.

'Sheriff wants to have a word with you.' He jerked his thumb in the direction of the half-open street door of the office.

Before Dave could speak, Keller said tightly: 'He's with me, Corran. I have important business with Mister Tremaine, business which can't wait. He'll be along when I've had a talk with him. Tell Salmon that from me.'

The deputy drew his lips back into a thin, hard smile. For a moment, his right hand hovered dangerously close to the butt of his gun as he stared at the tall, imperious figure of the doctor. The thought of action showed in his eyes. Then he switched his gaze to Dave, let his eyes wander up and down the tall figure, saw the smooth butt of the gun in the holster, thought better of anything, said: 'I hate to inconvenience you, mister. I'll tell Ben you'll be along in a little while.' Then, as if to salve what little was left of his dignity, he added: 'Better not try to leave town first, though.'

'I'll remember that,' Dave said easily. Deliberately, he turned his back on the other, fell into step beside Keller. 'Who was that *hombre*?' he asked when they were out of earshot.

'Pete Corran. One of Ben Salmon's deputies.'

'Salmon the Sheriff in Fenton?'

Keller nodded. 'That's right. He's been here for a couple of years now.'

'What happened to Bill Fox, who used to be lawman in town?'

The doctor looked up alertly at him. 'You remember Bill?' he said, his tone interested.

'Sure. He was the Sheriff when I was last in Fenton. Seemed like a good, honest lawman to me.'

'He was.' Bitterness edged the other's tone. 'That's why he was shot. There ain't any proof that it was Sabine who had a hand in it. Nobody seems to know what happened. Bill rode out one day to trail down some Mexican killer who was supposed to be in the neighbourhood. When his mount came back alone at nightfall a posse was formed and went out to look for him. They found his body in a small valley yonder in the hills. He'd been shot down from cover, never had a chance. Wasn't much later that Salmon was elected to the post. The talk is that Sabine arranged his election, that the ballot was rigged. One thing is for sure, he takes his orders from Sabine.'

'If there's anythin' I hate, it's a crooked lawman,' Dave gritted.

'You'll never prove anything as far as Salmon is concerned. He's far too clever for that.' Keller paused in front of the surgery, opened the door and led the way inside.

There was a sparsely furnished room at the front of the building, containing a desk littered with papers and a cupboard filled with bottles. Keller waved Tremaine to the chair in front of the desk, seated himself in the other after tossing his hat into one corner. He poured out a couple of drinks and slid a glass towards Dave.

'There's been some talk in town about you, Tremaine,' said Keller slowly. He eyed the other over the rim of his glass. 'They say that you were a fast man with a gun when you were last in town, a real hell-rider. From what Fordyce told me and the rumours I've heard about you from time to time, I'd say that reputation has been well earned.'

Dave shrugged as he produced the makings of a cigarette and began to roll one between his fingers. 'So you've heard rumours,' he said flatly. 'But what has that got to do with Luke Corrie and the shootin' of my pard?'

Keller leaned forward over the top of the desk, his hands flat on the scratched surface. 'Quite a lot, believe me. I know somethin' of what makes a gunman like you react the way he does. Lightning fast reflexes, ready to shoot first and ask questions later. Trouble is that once you've made your play there ain't any way of retrieving the situation if you happen to gun down the wrong man. I'm here to try to stop you from doin' just that.'

Dave sighed, sat back and lit the cigarette. He blew smoke in front of him, then said softly: 'Go ahead with what you want to say, Doc. The least I can do is listen to what you have to say, specially as you seem to be the only man in Fenton who'll tell me anythin' about Clem's death.'

Keller nodded. He placed the tips of his fingers together. 'Like I said, Clem was dead when I got to him. I'd say he'd been dead for about half an hour before I arrived on the scene. Some rider had spotted him lyin' in the alley, figured he was drunk but had gone to take a look. He came a-runnin' for the Sheriff soon as he found out who it was and what had happened.'

'And you went along?'

'Sure. He'd been shot in the back. There were a couple of slugs deep inside him and either one could've killed him. We had a good took around for any sign of the killer. We didn't expect to find anythin'. We all figured that whoever had shot him would be miles away by then. Then we stumbled on Luke Corrie. He was lyin' at the end of the alley, dead drunk. There were two shots fired from his gun, and fired only recently. The smell of burnt powder was strong in the barrel. The upshot was that Ben Salmon was forced to take him off to jail and charge him with murder.'

'So what happened? Seems to me he wasn't taken out and strung up?'

'No, he wasn't. Sabine rode into town and had a private talk with the Sheriff. When he rode out, Luke Corrie was with him.'

Dave nodded his head slowly, stared at the other through the curtain of blue smoke. 'If that's so, what makes you so goddamn certain that Corrie ain't Clem's killer?'

'Because I saw Luke just after they'd found him. I'll stake my reputation as a doctor that he couldn't have fired at anybody in the condition he was in. He'd just as easily have shot himself as some other man in that drunken state. Those two bullets that had killed Fordyce had been fired quickly and accurately and not by a man who was drunk.'

Dave rubbed his chin thoughtfully. His forehead was wrinkled in concentration. What the other said made sense. In spite of his anger, he was forced to recognize this.

'You see now why I had to talk to you,' Keller went on. 'A man like you rarely stops to think. You would have scoured the town for Luke Corrie and shot him down before he had a chance to speak for himself. And the trouble is that he honestly believes that he killed Fordyce. That's the real hold that Sabine has on him now.'

The tremendous Texas sunblast, filtering down on to the blistered paint surfaces of Fenton, burned on Dave's arms and shoulders as he made his way slowly along the street

in the direction of the Sheriff's office. A mangy dog lay in
the middle of the dusty street, legs thrust out in front of it,
tongue lolling from its open mouth as it panted in the
heat, too tired, or too lazy to get up and move.out of the
sun.

The Sheriff's office was a low-roofed building, standing a little apart from those on either side of it and at the
rear, the walls of the jail were of brick, not wood. Sheriff
Ben Salmon was seated in the high-backed chair behind
the paper-littered desk when Dave strode in, his legs up
on the desk, hands folded on his not insubstantial
paunch. Dave had rarely seen a man who looked so
unlike a lawman.

The other had his hat tilted over his face but he
pushed it back with a quick gesture as Dave went inside,
closing the door behind him. Pleasantly enough,
Tremaine said: 'Your deputy mentioned you had somethin' on your mind about me, Sheriff. Reckoned I'd
better come in and got it straightened out for you, whatever it is.'

Dropping his legs to the floor, Salmon stiffened a little
in his chair. His fleshy jowls shivered a little whenever he
moved his head and his eyes were set deep against the side
of his nose. His eyes, a pale blue, protruded a little from
their sockets, so that his face bore a perpetually startled
look, as if he were continually looking at something which
surprised him immensely. To Tremaine's way of thinking,
the other looked exactly like the many other crooked men
he had seen in the position of town Sheriff, whenever rich
and influential cattlemen wanted to manage politics in the
town.

Salmon's gaze travelled over Dave as he walked noncha-
lantly forward and seated himself, unasked, in the vacant
chair facing the lawman. For a moment, the other seemed
on the point of saying something sharply to him, then he
thought better of it, clamped his lips tight in a sorely tried
expression.

'Your name Dave Tremaine?' he muttered. 'Where'd

you come from and what's your business in Fenton?'

Carelessly, Dave said: 'I've ridden up from Tucson and points west. Take your pick of a score of towns. As for my business here, I reckon that's somethin' to do with me and no one else.'

Salmon leaned his bulk forward over the desk, eyes drawn down to mere slits. 'Better watch that sort of talk, mister. Otherwise I may have to put you in jail on suspicion.'

'Suspicion of what?'

'You rode in over the desert trail and crossed the Smoky some time last evening. You were met by Virginia Corrie and rode with her to her father's place. Then you rode into Fenton this mornin'.'

'Is that supposed to be against the law?' Dave asked pointedly.

'All depends on what your business is in this part of the territory. Could be that you're here to make trouble and if that's so, then I'm warnin' you right now that I'll arrest you and lock you up the first move you make in town that I don't like.'

Dave glanced at the other curiously. Evidently Salmon was believing that he had the backing of Sabine and his crew in any action he took and that no man, however fast and dangerous he was with a gun would stand up to the whole Sabine crew.

'A friend of mine was shot in the back here a while ago. He wrote me a letter tellin' me of the fact that he'd struck it rich up in the hills on the edge of town, but that he was scared somebody was tryin' to kill him. I rode out here fast as I could. Seems I got here a mite too late. Clem Fordyce is buried up yonder in the churchyard.'

He saw the hardening of the sheriff's face at Clem's name, the deepening of the lines around the edges of the lawman's mouth and the corners of his eyes.

'All that happened some weeks ago,' Salmon said sharply, tersely. 'We held an inquiry right away. If you heard that Fordyce was shot in the back then you heard wrong, mister. It was a case of self-defence.'

Dave raised has brows a little. 'Sorry,' he said eventually, 'but I don't believe you. I've heard from two men who had no call to be involved personally in this and they both say he was shot twice in the back and his gun was put into his fist after he was dead.'

'You goin' to believe their word, or mine?' challenged the other.

Dave grinned, but there was no hint of mirth in his smile as he faced the other down. 'You know damned well what the answer is to that, Sheriff. Too many funny things happenin' around Fenton for my likin'. Besides, I've got Clem's word for it, even if he is dead and can't speak none for himself.'

'You callin me a liar?'

Dave shrugged again. 'If I'm wrong, I'll take it all back when I find out the truth.'

'You won't be doin' any apologizin', to me or anybody else.' He heaved himself heavily from the chair and stood up, glaring down at Dave as if the increased height over the sitting man, gave him an added confidence. 'You're headin' out of town before sundown or I'll put you in jail. I—' He broke off sharply, his voice trailing away into an uneasy silence as Dave rose slowly to his feet.

'Seems to me you're doin' a lot of talkin', Sheriff,' Dave said, his tone pleasant but with a noticeable undertone of menace which was not lost on the other. 'I didn't come here to start trouble, but if it comes, then I'm more'n ready to meet it halfway. Your killers are goin' to find it a little more difficult – and dangerous – to try to shoot me in the back without warnin'. Besides, I don't take threats, especially from crooked lawmen. I've met your kind before, in plenty of cowtowns, Salmon. Men who do the biddin' of the big ranchers who need to bend the law to their own ends.'

'Why you . . . you,' spluttered Salmon. A red flush rose into his beefy features, staining his thick, bull-like neck.

'Take it easy, Sheriff.' Dave thrust his face forward until it was only a few inches from the other's. 'You're not doin' your blood pressure any good gettin' on your high horse like this.'

Turning on his heel, he walked contemptuously to the door, opening it and slamming it behind him. Outside, Corran, the deputy, stood lounging against the wall. He straightened up a little as Dave came out, pulled the piece of straw from between his lips, said conversationally: 'You have your talk with Ben, mister?'

Dave turned sharply on him. 'Let's say I gave him my point of view,' he said abruptly, then mellowed as he realized that he had no evidence that the deputy was in the same dirty business as the Sheriff. 'Where's the best saloon and hotel?'

'Reckon the Broken Lance yonder has the best beer.' The deputy pointed. 'The Trail's End is the hotel for you. In the square yonder.'

'Thanks, friend.' Dave stepped down into the street, made his way to the Broken Lance saloon. His first need was for a cool beer to slake the thirst that was in him. There would be plenty of time to get a bed for himself. Pushing open the batwing doors with the flat of his hands, he stepped inside. It was dim and cool in the body of the saloon and there were several customers, some at tables playing cards, others standing at the long bar.

Casually, Dave let his glance slide around the long room, taking in everything. The three men who stood in a tight little bunch at the far end of the bar looked round sharply as he walked in. Most of the other men there resumed what they were doing a few moments after eyeing him up and down casually, but not these three men. They continued to watch him closely as he stepped over to the bar.

There was a thin sneer on the face of the short, stocky man with the twin Colts slung low on his hips. Sled Cantry was a professional killer. When he was young he had killed for many different reasons, for hatred, for money, for the sheer joy it gave him, the pleasure of marking up another thin notch on the handle of his Colt. Then the law had begun to take an interest in him and there had been a period when he had ridden hard and ridden fast, striving to keep one jump ahead of the men who were hunting him down. Not until a couple of years before had he finally ridden into Fenton, a town that was growing fast and where the law was vested in one man – Jed Sabine. He had realized that, of necessity, he would have to stop running some time and some place, and Fenton seemed to him to be the ideal place for this. The money which Sabine had offered to keep him on the payroll as a professional killer, had been far more than he had ever earned before. He thought about the meeting he had had with Jed Sabine two hours before. The job he had been given was the most lucrative yet.

Draining the whiskey from his glass he looked along the bar at Tremaine. He had heard nothing about this man, but he liked to appraise every man he was to kill. For years now, his livelihood had been earned from his gunskill and he was not a man to step into gunplay lightly. If he considered that there might be a chance of his opponent outdrawing him, he was not averse to doing it any way he thought fit, even to shooting a man in the back from cover. But Sabine had been adamant in this case. He wanted as many people in Fenton to know that Tremaine had been killed by one of his hired gunmen.

As he let his gaze wander over the tall figure of the man standing against the bar, a slight frown creased his forehead. He noticed the single gun which the other wore, low on his hip, and he felt a sense of momentary surprise as he saw that the other was left-handed. It was just possible that Tremaine was one of the few men who favoured the cross draw, but somehow, noting the man's stance, he doubted it. He shook his head quickly to dislodge the sudden thought which had popped into his mind, filled the glass again from the tall bottle in front of him.

'That Tremaine?' he said in a very soft voice.

Forest gave a brief nod. 'That's him,' he affirmed. 'You sure can take him. I've heard that he's devil fast with a gun.'

'Where'd you hear that?' Cantry asked casually.

'There's talk that he's ridden up from the border some place. Could be he ain't the same man, but—'

'Makes no difference to me who he is,' said Cantry confidently. His face resumed its normal cruel expression. He raised his voice a little so that Tremaine could hear. 'I reckon I can outdraw any man in this saloon.'

Dave did not turn his head but continued to stare straight ahead of him. In the long mirror that stretched along the whole length of the wall behind the bar, he could see every man in the saloon. Some of the card players had flicked quick glances at the man who had spoken and he could feel the atmosphere in the saloon grow taut and electric.

The bartender came along the bar as Dave held up a finger, poured out a second glass for him. Bending forward the man said softly: 'I ain't seen you in this place before, mister, have I?'

Dave shook his head. 'No.' He sipped his drink slowly. 'Ain't been in Fenton for some years now.'

'You here on business?'

Dave's eyes glinted a little as he eyed the other up and down. He saw the look on the man's face.

'Don't get me wrong, mister.' The bartender spoke without moving his lips much, as if anxious that nobody else in the saloon should see him talking to Dave. 'But it seems to me there's goin' to be trouble with Cantry yonder. He's a bad one. I don't aim to get this place shot up and that's where his kind of talk is goin' to lead.'

'Cantry, you say. He one of Jed Sabine's men?' A vague suspicion was beginning to grow in Dave's mind.

'That's right. Sabine hired him a couple of years ago. Brought him in from some place down south, I heard.'

Dave grinned tightly. 'Could be you're right and he's lookin' for trouble. If he is, then I'm willin' to oblige him.' Dave had spoken loudly so that everyone in the saloon could hear his words. Behind the bartender, reflected in the mirror, he could see the sudden stiffening of Cantry's body, the way the man's mouth became pinched down, eyes slitted a little.

The bartender allowed his jaw to sag open a little at the other's temerity. It was very seldom that anyone came into the saloon and spoke openly like this where Cantry was concerned. Such a man would have to be either crazy or drunk and as far as he could make out, the man who faced him across the bar was neither. He uttered a faint sigh, turned his head and glanced along the rear of the bar to where the sawed-off shotgun he always kept for emergencies such as this, reposed a few feet away. Dave noticed the other's glance, said harshly.

'I wouldn't make a move for that gun you've got stashed away there, mister. I'm just as liable to blow your head off as that of any other man in this room.'

The bartender stared straight into Dave's face and didn't like what he saw mirrored there. He had met up with plenty of tough men in his time, thought he knew the ways in which most of them acted, but there was something about the man in front of him that sent a little chill down his back and made him forget all about that shotgun as he stepped back to where the empty, polished glasses were set up neatly along the rear of the bar.

A few yards away, Cantry had turned his head, placed his half-empty glass on the bar. His features were set into vicious lines as he edged a couple of feet away from the bar, his arms swinging loosely by his sides.

'Your name Tremaine?' Cantry asked, his small animal eyes bright in his face.

'That's right.'

'Just wanted to make sure I'm killin' the right man,' said the other softly.

'You workin' for Jed Sabine, or is this somethin' personal?' Dave asked.

Cantry uttered a harsh laugh. He did not remove his gaze from Dave's face for a single instant. 'Ain't nothin' personal in it, Tremaine,' he muttered. 'I just do this for the money.'

'And those two *hombres* standin' at the back of you?' Dave spoke slowly and deliberately. 'They makin' this play with you? If they ain't, then I suggest they step away from the bar, otherwise I'm likely to gun them down too.'

He saw instantly that his words had the desired effect. For a moment he had wondered if he had to take on all three men. Fast as he was, he doubted if he would have been able to kill them before being killed himself. Now he saw the sudden blanching on the face of the big man, knew that he did not consider himself a gunfighter. The shorter man, too, moved suddenly away from the bar, edging back towards one of the tables, leaving Cantry alone.

'I don't need men to back up my play, Tremaine,' snarled Cantry viciously.

Dave nodded. Normally, the loose ties which existed between any group of outlaws would have been sufficient for these three men to fan out so that they might take him from three directions. Cantry had crouched slightly, his hands hovering just above the butts of the guns in his belt, fingers clawed like the talons of an eagle as they shadowed his guns.

In those few moments, aware of the deep silence in the saloon, Dave felt as if everything were curiously magnified for him. He could hear the faint sound of a horse in the far distance, somewhere beyond the windows, heard the ticking of the tall clock that stood in one corner of the bar.

'You're makin' a big mistake right now, tryin' to

outdraw me,' Cantry said. He spoke in a high-pitched tone. 'I've killed more men than you can remember.'

'You settin' to bore me to death with your talk,' Dave said thinly. The insult in his voice made the other flush slightly and he saw that the barb had gone home.

Sucking in a sharp breath, the other clicked his teeth tightly together. For a moment his gaze drifted away from Dave's face, towards the bar just behind Tremaine. Dave grinned. It was an old trick, he knew. The other was hoping to divert his attention just long enough to give himself an added advantage for the draw. Switching his gaze back to Dave, Cantry's hands moved, striking down for his guns. Cantry's draw was the fastest of all the men on Jed Sabine's payroll, the guns seemed to leap from their holsters into his hands as if by magic ; but the onlookers in the saloon saw the first stab of flame spurt from the single gun in Tremaine's left hand, saw Cantry stagger and lurch as the heavy slug took him full in the chest. A spasm went through his body and of their own volition, his fingers squeezed down on the triggers of his guns, one bullet driving deeply into the wooden floor in front of his twisting body, the other smashing a bottle on the shelf at the back of the bar. Dave fired again, his gun coughing smoke and lead and Cantry went back, shoulders hitting the edge of one of the card tables, smashing it beneath his crumpling weight as he fell. His hat fell off as he bounced on the floor, hair glinting a little in the shaft of sunlight that struck down through the window on to his upturned face. Dave knew that the other had been dead long before he had hit the floor. There was crimson staining the front of the gunman's shirt and two ugly, round holes punched into it.

Turning slowly, Dave said in a harsh voice: 'Anybody else want to step up and try?'

Nobody made any reply and with a movement almost of contempt, he thrust the Colt back into the leather holster, moved over to the bar and downed the rest of his drink. He was in the act of pouring out another when the swing doors were thrust open and Salmon came in with Corran, the deputy, close on his heels. The Sheriff had his gun out, stared about him as he came into the room, then his eyes lit on the sprawled body of the man near the table. Going over to him, he bent, peered down into the upturned face, the wide-open, vacant eyes and said in a faintly awed tone: 'It's Cantry – Sabine's top gun.'

'That's right,' Dave said quietly. 'He admitted himself that Sabine had paid him to kill me. Trouble was, he didn't bother to find out if I was faster than him or not.'

Salmon straightened. He did not holster his gun, but strode towards Dave, his face grim. 'I warned you only a little while ago what would happen if you started trouble in town, mister. Seems you didn't heed my warnin'.'

Dave nodded in the direction of the dead man. 'He drew first,' he said thinly. 'There were plenty of witnesses to that.'

Salmon whirled. 'All right, you men,' he called loudly. 'You all saw this. What happened?'

For a moment there was silence in the saloon, then the big man who had been standing with Cantry when Dave had entered the saloon, said hoarsely: 'That ain't the truth he's tellin', Ben. He never gave Cantry a chance. Shot him down without warnin'. Cantry just managed to get his gun free when the bullets hit him. You know yourself how fast Cantry was. This *hombre* wouldn't have had a chance against him if it had been an even fight.'

Dave drew in a sharp breath. So that was how things were going to be. He guessed, looking around at the faces of the bartender and the card players at the tables that he could not expect them to back up his story. Sabine would make things bad for them if they sided with him.

'That's right, Sheriff.' The bartender spoke up. 'This *hombre* came in and started askin' questions. Seemed hell-bent for trouble, if you ask me. Then he started talkin' provocative like, tryin' to needle Cantry into a fight.'

Salmon nodded. He lined the Colt upon Dave's chest. 'I figured it that way when I first met up with you, Tremaine. We don't hold with killers in Fenton. I'm takin' you in with me. If you want to make a try for your gun, then go ahead. Nothin' would give me greater pleasure than gunnin' down a stinkin' polecat like you.'

Dave straightened, stood away from the bar. He knew that the other meant every word he said, knew that he had no chance at all of squeezing off even one shot before the Sheriff pulled the trigger, yet in spite of this, the thought of action was in his mind. He stared at the other critically. 'You know why these men are sayin' this, Sheriff. They daren't go against Sabine. They're frightened for their own lives if they speak the truth.'

'I said *git*,' snapped Salmon. He prodded the barrel of his gun into Dave's ribs to emphasize his warning, reached out to pull the Colt from Dave's holster with his free hand.

Before he could do so, a voice from the top of the stairs said sharply: 'Leave that gun alone, Salmon, and stand away from him.'

Dave felt a sudden sense of surprise. Switching his gaze from Salmon's face, he glanced up to the head of the stairs. The woman who stood there was probably in her thirties, although it was difficult to tell exactly, because of the paint and powder she wore. Her red, flared dress stood out starkly against the drab back-ground, but more important than that was the short-barrelled Winchester she held in her hands, the weapon pointed so that it was levelled at Ben Salmon but could be easily and rapidly switched to cover any man in the saloon below.

Salmon stepped back from Dave. He said harshly: 'Now see here, Roxanna, you can't go buttin' in on the law like this, I—'

'You'll do nothing until you've heard what I have to say.' There was a note of naked scorn in her voice. 'I'm not afraid of speaking out the truth even if the rest of those cowards down there are. I saw everything that happened.

That man is telling the truth. Cantry started the fight. He even said that Sabine had paid him well for the job of killing him. And it was Cantry who drew first, only this time, he came up against somebody a mite faster with a gun than he was.'

Salmon thrust out his tongue and ran it over dry lips. He said blusteringly to the girl. 'You don't know what you're saying, Roxanna. Now put up that gun before you get hurt. I don't want to have to put you in jail too for obstructin' the law, but I will if you don't do as I tell you.'

Roxanna laughed shrilly. 'Obstructing the law.' She shook her head. 'There is no law in Fenton except that which Sabine dispenses. You're just hiding behind that star, Salmon, scared to do your job properly. You're no better than the rest of those yellow-livered, spineless creatures down there who call themselves men.'

Dave saw Salmon flush, but noticed that the other had lowered his gun. Evidently the Sheriff had decided that there was no point in risking his life, even if it was a woman who was holding that gun. Certainly the girl looked as if she was quite capable of using the rifle if it came to a showdown, but Dave knew that she could not hope to stop all of these men if they decided to throw in their lot with Salmon.

'You're not doin' yourself any good talkin' like this,' Salmon said. He had forced a calmer note into his voice, 'Besides, this *hombre* is just a killer who's ridden into town from somewhere near the border. You don't want to side with him. He'll bring you nothin' but trouble.'

Out of the corner of his eye, Dave glanced across the saloon. It occurred to him that the sheriff must have some reason for continuing to talk like this. It did not take him long to see what it was. One of the men had risen quietly and unobtrusively from the furthest table and was making his way cautiously along the far wall towards the side of the stairs, out of sight of the girl at the top.

The man had already drawn his gun, was edging

forward to get in a shot at the girl when Dave drew his own, slammed down hard with the barrel across the sheriff's wrist, causing him to drop his gun with a sudden howl of pain and rage. The man standing near the far wall turned his head at the sudden commotion and in the same instant, Dave fired. With a wild yell, the gunman dropped his weapon and clutched at his smashed wrist. Sheriff Salmon turned on Dave, his face red with anger.

'Just hold it right there, Sheriff,' Dave said coldly. 'I figure you've shown your hand right now. Nobody's takin' me in until I finish what I came here to do. Maybe Cantry yonder was the *hombre* who shot Clem Fordyce in the back on Sabine's orders, maybe not. But I aim to find out and no crooked lawman is goin' to stop me.'

'You can't buck the law like this,' Salmon spluttered.

Dave grinned viciously, gave the other a shove that sent him sprawling along the front of the bar until he crashed against one of the tables. 'There's no law in Fenton,' he said harshly. 'Not when the sheriff is in cahoots with Jed Sabine.'

Out of the edge of his vision, he saw Corran reach for his gun. Dave gave him no chance. Swinging sideways with his right hand, he hit him in the mouth, sending him staggering backwards, arms flailing helplessly. Corran rolled over on the floor, put up his hand to his mouth, holding it, the blood spurting through his fingers as he rocked back and forth on his heels, moaning softly through his smashed lips where his teeth had bitten deeply into them.

Turning to Salmon, Dave said thinly: 'Get on your feet and get out of here. The same goes for the rest of Sabine's crew. Better take that body with you. And if anybody has the idea of tryin' to stop me like they did Clem Fordyce, they'd better think again.'

He saw the girl at the top of the stairs watching him as the men near the bar began to drift out of the saloon. Two of them picked up the dead body of Cantry and took him out. At the door, Salmon paused, looked back, glaring at him. He said harshly: 'You won't get away with this, Tremaine. Don't think you can buck the whole town and get off scot free.'

When he had gone, Dave turned back to the bar, picked up his unfinished drink. The girl came slowly down the stairs, laid the Winchester on the top of the bar and said softly: 'Don't I deserve a drink after saving your life?'

'Sure, Ma'am.' Dave motioned to the bartender. The girl was smiling pleasantly but he had the vague feeling that he should be careful with her. There was a faintly-noticeable hardness in her which showed through the softness of her features.

He said: 'You really mean what you said back there, that you would have shot those men, includin' the Sheriff?'

'They wouldn't have gone for their guns,' she said quietly. 'I know those men of old. They talk a lot, but they never do anythin' unless they have the drop on you.'

Dave raised his brows a little. 'You talk like someone who's used to handlin' a gun,' he said.

She nodded and a curiously speculative look came into her eyes. 'I didn't always sing and dance in a place like this for a living,' she said. Her face assumed a hard expression. 'We had a ranch and more than three thousand head of cattle until a few years ago. Not far from Fenton. Then Sabine and his men moved in and started to take over everything. My father tried to stand out against him.' Her eyes clouded a little at the memory. Downing the drink in front of her in a single gulp, she went on: 'Sabine knew he'd never get my father to sell out to him and in those days he couldn't risk an open fight – it was before he brought in these hired killers like Cantry – so he had to do his dirty work discreetly, make things look like an accident. One night my father didn't get back from town after he'd ridden in for supplies. I hitched up the spare team and went to look for him. I found him halfway along the trail near the river. The bridge had collapsed just as he was driving over it, pitching him into the water. He was pinned under the wagon and drowned.'

'I see.' Dave nodded sympatheically. 'But how can you be so certain that this was Sabine's doin'?'

'Oh, I know it looked like an accident, but a couple of days later I went back and took a look around. The support of the bridge had been sawn almost completely through. They were fresh saw marks. Evidently it had been done just before my father came to the bridge on his way back. Three days later, before he was even cold in his grave, Sabine came and made what he said was his final offer for the ranch and the cattle. He warned me that I'd never be able to run the place single-handed, that none of the hands would stay and work for me if I tried to keep the place going.'

She pushed her empty glass towards the bartender, waited until it was filled again, sipped it slowly, eyeing Dave over the rim. The hardness was still there in her face, making her look older than she was. 'I thought he was just talking at first. But it didn't take me long to find out that he was telling the truth. I don't know what sort of hold he had over the men who'd worked for my father. But one by one, they took their wages and drifted on over the hill. Even Cookie left in the end. It was impossible for me to think of keeping going without any help at all. Then the bank asked for payment of the mortgage. It wasn't due for another three months, but they said they had to get in the money otherwise they would be forced to foreclose on the ranch. I tried everywhere to find someone who would lend me the money, to tide me over, but there was no one. The next day, Sabine came back, said he had heard I was in difficulties and made me another offer for the ranch. This time, it was only a little more than half of his previous offer, but there was nothing else I could do.'

'So you had to sell out to him at a loss.'

'A big loss,' she admitted. 'Ever since then I've been trying to prove that Sabine was behind my father's death.

But you know as well as I do that Salmon is in Sabine's pay. He refuses to do anything to help.'

'So now you have to sing and dance in this saloon.'

She nodded slowly, drained her glass. 'Don't feel sorry for me, mister. That's one thing I can't take. Sooner or later, I'm going to pay back Sabine for all he's done to me. Right now, he figures that I'm harmless. But as for you, now that you've shot down his best gunman, he won't rest until you're dead. He'll have to get rid of you before you can bring him any more trouble. I figure your best plan would be to ride out of town and keep on riding.'

'Not until I find out who killed Clem Fordyce. He was a friend of mine and I mean to find his murderer. When I've done that, maybe I'll take your advice.'

The girl eyed him steadily for a long moment, then she ran the tip of her tongue around her lips. There was a speculative look in her eyes. 'They say it was Luke Corrie who shot Fordyce in the back,' she said slowly, and with deliberateness.

'Do you believe that?'

She shrugged her bare shoulders. 'I don't see any reason not to believe it. Corrie is one of Sabine's men and he was arrested for the shooting. Then Sabine rode into town, talked things over with Salmon and the upshot of that was that Corrie was released and rode off with Sabine and the rest of his men. If he wasn't guilty, why did Salmon release him like that?'

'I'm not sure,' murmured Dave reflectively. 'That's somethin' that has been puzzlin' me for a while now.'

'You think it may have been somebody else who did the killing?' Roxanna asked him curiously. It seemed that this was the first time such a possibility had occurred to her. She narrowed her eyes a little in thought. 'Everybody knows that Corrie had sworn to kill Fordyce, but I reckon that goes for plenty of others in Fenton as well. Fordyce had a big gold strike up there in the hills and there was scarcely a man in town who wouldn't have murdered him to find that claim.'

'I'll remember that,' Dave said slowly. He put his glass down on the bar, shook his head as the bartender came forward. Stepping away, he said softly: 'Better keep that rifle handy, Roxanne. I doubt if Salmon will forgive you for what you did today.'

She lifted her chin imperiously. 'I know how to handle him,' she said thinly. 'He won't try anything.'

Dave walked over to the doors, stepped out on to the boardwalk. There was still a lot of heat in the air and the glare of the sunlight washing down over the town was a punishing thing that hurt the eyes and brought a throbbing ache to the back of his forehead. He threw a quick look up and down the street but there was no sign of Salmon or any of the men who had been in the saloon earlier. He guessed that perhaps word had gone back to Sabine that Cantry had failed in his task. Smiling grimly to himself, he stepped down into the street, made his way along the road to the square. He would need to get himself a meal and a bed.

FOUR

HELL ERUPTS

Jed Sabine sat on the ranch house porch, staring out into the gathering dusk as the reds and golds on the sunset were swamped by the deep purples of night sweeping in from the east. He felt the silence around him, drew down on his thoughts. He felt oddly restless and dissatisfied. The coming of this man Tremaine had something to do with it, he felt sure. Just why the other should represent such a menace to him, he did not know. He had never been afraid of one man ever since he had built up the biggest spread in this part of the territory and brought in enough men to help him protect it. There would always be men anxious to move in on him and try to wrest away from him that which he had made, but he felt confident he could fight them all off. Why then should he feel so unsure about this man Tremaine?

At first, he couldn't put his finger on any possible reason, but it became apparent before long, once he started to think seriously about it. Why he had allowed Forrest to go out after that old coot, Fordyce, he did not know. It had taken a lot of string pulling to get Corrie off the hook, but once it had been done, it had come to him that everything had turned out for the best. The fact that Corrie owed him close on three thousand dollars, that he had the other IOUs had been only a slender hold over the other. Now he had this to keep Corrie working for him.

It had not been difficult to get the other drunk that night, fire off a couple of bullets from his guns, then knock him out and place him in the alley only a few yards from Fordyce's body. Even Corrie firmly believed that he had killed the other.

Now, however, this man Tremaine had butted in, was noseying around town, asking questions, probing into things which were best left hidden. Sooner or later, if he wasn't stopped, he would find out something of the truth and even if he was killed, Corrie would know he was not a murderer. Lighting a cheroot, he puffed on it for several minutes. It was rapidly growing darker now and the first of the sky sentinels showed in the east, gleaming brightly against the clear sky.

Tossing the cheroot on to the ground, he got heavily to his feet, walked out over the courtyard to the corral. He had expected Cantry and the others to arrive back before now with the news that Tremaine was no longer around to trouble him. When he hadn't arrived by sundown, he had got to thinking that maybe something had gone wrong, that perhaps Tremaine hadn't shown up in town as they had expected, or maybe he had slipped into town and then pulled out again, running back to the Corrie ranch with his tail between his legs. For a moment, the thought made him smile. Then he felt the sense of worry climb up in his mind again. If Tremaine had run like that, it would not help him. He would still be around, still potentially dangerous.

Disturbed, he began to pace restlessly back and forth along the perimeter fence of the corral. The horses moved around in the centre, milling togther.

When he heard the quiet run of horses along the trail that led over the hill towards town, he stiffened abruptly, turned and stared off into the darkness, striving to pick them out long before they were visible against the looming bulk of the hill. He heard them come on, knew that there were more than one.

There came the faintly echoing clatter of hooves as they rode over the wooden bridge that spanned the small stream and a few minutes later they rode down into the courtyard, the riders swinging stiffly from their saddles and moving their mounts towards the corral. Going forward, Sabine called: 'Who is that?'

Forrest's voice came back a few moments later. 'Just us, boss,' he called. Sabine stepped forward a couple of paces, saw the two shadows loom up in front of him. *Only two.* He said at once: 'Cantry not with you?'

'Cantry's dead,' Forrest said slowly. He opened the gate of the corral and let his mount through, sliding off the saddle as he did so, hanging it on the nearby post.

Sabine sucked in a sharp breath. He stepped right up to the other, his hand gripping the foreman's arm in a vice-like grip. He said through tight-clenched teeth: 'What do you mean that Cantry's dead? What happened in town? I sent you there with a chore to do, to kill Tremaine.'

Forrest stared down at him stonily, then said thinly: 'Tremaine killed him. That *hombre* is devil fast with a gun, faster than Cantry.'

With a tremendous effort, Sabine controlled his rage. 'And what did you do while he was outdrawin' Cantry? Just stand there and let him do it?'

Forrest was silent for a long moment, then he said tightly: 'I've done a lot of dirty work for you, Sabine. But if you think I'm goin' to commit suicide by steppin' up against a man like Tremaine, then you're wrong.'

'You figurin' on runnin' out on me, Forrest?' There was a note of glacial menace in Sabine's voice. Some of it got through to the foreman. He hesitated for a moment, then swallowed thickly, his Adam's apple bobbing up and down in his throat. 'I ain't thinkin' of anythin' like that,' he said tightly. 'But I know none of us have any chance against this *hombre*, Tremaine, in an even fight. That's all I'm sayin'.'

'There's more ways of killin' a coyote than catchin' him in a trap,' Sabine said harshly. He stood in silent debate with himself for several minutes. 'Where is Tremaine now?'

'Still in town, I reckon. Salmon came in and tried to arrest him for killin' Cantry.'

'And what happened?'

'That dame Roxanne stepped in with a Winchester. Weren't nothin' we could do. She had us all dead to rights. I'm damned sure she'd have shot the first man to go for his gun.'

'So you let a woman run you out of the Broken Lance.' Scorn edged Sabine's voice. He let his words hang in the stillness. 'What kind of men have I hired?'

Forrest looked uncomfortable, but said nothing. After an uneasy pause, Sabine said: 'It looks as if I'll have to get myself a fast gun. Until then, I'll pass the word along to Corrie that Tremaine knows he was the man who shot Fordyce and unless he wants to die himself, he'd better fix Tremaine – and fast.'

'You reckon the kid will fall for that?'

Sabine grinned. 'He already thinks he did the killin'. When he hears what sort of man Tremaine is, he'll do anythin' to kill this *hombre* before he gets a bullet himself. If he shoots Tremaine in the back, guess it won't be any skin off my nose. As for you—' He glanced levelly at the foreman, 'I think you had better keep in mind the fact that you were the man who shot Fordyce in the back. A word in the right ear and Tremaine will come gunnin' for you.'

Forrest said nothing but there was a tight, worried look on his face as he turned away and made his way over to the bunkhouse.

In his room at the front of the hotel, Dave cleaned up and shaved, then went down into the dining-room for supper. He doubted now if Salmon intended to try anything more again, certainly not until he had received fresh orders from Jed Sabine, but in spite of this, Dave chose the table furthest from the door, his back to the wall, where he could watch everybody who came into the room.

The meal, when it came, was well cooked and he ate ravenously. When he had finished, he sat where he was, sitting back in his chair, letting his muscles relax, content to smoke a cigarette and watch the other people in the room. He had felt tired when he had made his way up to his room an hour before, but the food had acted as a stimulant, together with the two cups of black coffee and he now felt restlessness bubbling up inside him, the desire to go out and try to find out more about Clem's death.

Little incidents of the past weeks kept coming into his mind; images of the past and in spite of every effort he made to ignore them, they persisted in intruding upon his consciousness. The smell of a wood fire in his nostrils, the sight of the yeasty ferment of the star-strewn heavens seen from among the tall pines on the side of the mountain, the scar-like trail as it wound in and out of sand-blown rocks etched into strange and fantastic shapes by the wind. Fully enjoying the luxury and the laziness of the rest which came after a long day, he had almost finished his cigarette when the door of the dining-room opened and a man came in. Dave recognized him instantly. It was Corran, the deputy sheriff. The other paused in the entrance for a moment, turning his head and looking curiously about him. Then his gaze rested on Dave and he hitched up his gunbelt a little around his middle and walked over.

Standing beside the table, he indicated the vacant chair opposite Dave. 'Mind if I sit down?' he asked, his tone pleasant enough. 'Got a few things I'd like to talk over with you.'

Dave hesitated, then nodded slowly. 'Go ahead,' he said quietly. Inwardly, he wondered what the other wanted with him. He searched the other's actions for some hidden motives, but could think of none.

'You sure knocked hell out of Sabine when you killed Cantry,' he said softly. There was a faint grin on his face. He rubbed his own mouth ruefully. 'You also pack quite a wallop with those fists of yours.'

Dave grinned. 'You take it nicely, Corran,' he said. 'But what's on your mind? Salmon send you over to repeat his warnin'?'

Corran shook his head. 'Nothin' like that,' he said, his tone serious. 'Sheriff don't know I'm over here talkin' to you. Doubt if he'd like it if he did know.'

'I see.' Tremaine murmured. He stared fixedly at the other.

'Things aren't goin' to be too good for you once Sabine hears of the shootin' this afternoon. He'll have to do somethin' about it, or the townsfolk might get to thinkin' that maybe he ain' the big man around these parts after all.'

'And that would be just too bad for him, wouldn't it?' Dave said pointedly.

'You're darned right, it would,' affirmed the other harshly. He lit a cigarette. 'He's built this empire of his on fear. Anybody shows himself able to stand up against him and folk might get around to thinkin' for themselves and turnin' on him.'

Dave knit his brows. 'Just why are you tellin' me all this?'

Corran stared down at the cigarette between his fingers for a long moment, the blue smoke curling up in front of has face. He pondered the question for a while. Presently, he said: 'I've got my reasons, Tremaine. Sure I'm deputy sheriff but that don't mean I agree with the way things are run around here. Besides, the last sheriff was my uncle. I'm near certain that Sabine had a hand in his death, but like most things that happen in and around Fenton, it isn't possible to prove it.'

'No, he's as cunning as a fox and as deadly as a rattler from what I've heard,' said Dave musingly. 'But all I came here for was to look up my friend Clem Fordyce. I'd already figgered that somethin' might have happened to him from what he wrote in his last letter. Now I find that he's dead and there's scarcely anyone in town who wants to tell me how it happened. Sabine means nothing to me. I've seen frontier towns like this that have been braced by the trail crews and I know what can happen. They leave a town smashed and burned. But that ain't any of my business unless I find that Sabine was the man who killed Clem or who ordered him killed.' He turned the last into a hopeful question.

Corran smoked for a few moments, then shrugged. 'I was there when Sabine rode in and ordered Salmon to release Luke Corrie. He reckoned that even if Corrie was responsible for the killin', nobody in Fenton was goin' to hold any of his men without his say-so. I guess that Ben was only too glad to let Corrie go. At least, it relieved him of the responsibility of having to decide what to do with him.'

'But you don't know for sure whether it was Corrie who did it or not?' Dave persisted.

Corran shook his head. 'I figure it could have been anybody. One thing is for sure. Luke swore he'd get Fordyce for somethin' he'd done. He was gettin' steadily more and more drunk the night that it happened. He could've done it I reckon.'

'Is Corrie the sort of man who would shoot another in the back rather than face him down?'

The deputy pressed his lips together into a tight line. 'Luke used to be a decent sort of fella before he got in with Sabine. There's talk that Luke fell in with some crooked card player in the saloon yonder and lost a heap of money. Sabine paid his debt, but took his IOUs as security. Weren't nothin' that Luke could do then but work for Sabine and hope to pay off the debt.'

'Any idea how much he owed Sabine?'

Corran shrugged his shoulders. 'Some say it was close on two thousand dollars.'

Dave let a low whistle go through his teeth. 'What was

the young fool thinkin' of, playing for stakes like that and with a crooked gambler?'

'Guess he was always a trifle hot-headed, but there was no real harm in him until Sabine got his claws into him.' Corran leaned forward a little over the table, lowered his voice still further. 'There was also somethin' between him and the dancing girl at the Broken Lance saloon.'

'Corrie and Roxanna?' Dave stared at the other in surprise. This little bit of information came as a distinct shock to him. Certainly Roxanna was a pretty girl, might look even prettier if she had all of that paint and powder off her face and he could imagine that she might make a beautiful enough picture to sway a man's heart, especially an impressionable one like Luke Corrie's.

'That surprise you?' inquired the other.

'A little,' Dave nodded slowly. The little bit of information was beginning to slip into place. Perhaps there was another reason why Roxanna evidently hated Jed Sabine so much. Perhaps it was also because of the change the other had wrought in Luke Corrie.

'Don't trust Roxanna too much.' There was a new expression at the back of Corran's eyes as he stared directly at Dave across the table. 'I know that she stepped in back there and maybe saved your life, but she didn't do it for you. She did it because she'll help anybody who might stand against Sabine. She hates him like poison. Reckon she has plenty of reasons.' He crushed out the butt of his cigarette, scraped back his chair and rose to his feet. 'Don't dig too deep into what goes on in this town, Tremaine,' he said deliberately. 'This ain't a threat, just a friendly warnin'. I've got no love for Sabine, but I've got enough sense and concern for my own hide, to know that there ain't anythin' anybody can do to stop him now.'

Dave drew back his lips over his teeth. 'Thanks for the warnin',' he said softly, 'but I wouldn't be too sure about Sabine. He's a man just like the rest of us and a bullet is no respector of people.'

Corran looked at him curiously for a long moment,

seemed on the point of saying something more, then obviously thought better of it, turned on his heel and walked out. Dave watched his retreating back until the other had disappeared through the door, then got up from the table and went out himself. He had the hunch that Corran had been on the level, that the other had spoken the truth. But it did not help him any. He could feel the deadly danger that lay all around him in this town. Maybe, he reckoned, it would be better for him if he rode out at sun-up and made his way back to the Corrie ranch. There, at least, he should be safe if only for a little while, time in which to make his plans and decide what he should do next.

It was cool out on the boardwalk and he stood at the corner of the square, watching the lights gleaming yellow in the buildings all about him, and the intermittent red glows from the cigarettes of the men in the shadows. A couple of men came riding along the main street, their horses' hooves kicking up the dry dust. In the long summer the street was a river of grey-white flowing dust that got everywhere during the daytime, but when the spring and autumn rains came, it would be transformed into a veritable quagmire, a muddy stream ankle-deep.

He fell to thinking how it might be in the future, if only the forces of law and order could triumph here. The railroad had come and this was usually the forerunner of prosperity for a town such as this, situated on the frontier. Already, the bounds of civilization were pushing steadily west, out clear to California and the Pacific. Nothing could stop the march of progress, although here and there, men tried. The trouble was that if law and order was not maintained in a small town such as this, very soon it drifted back into an empty shell as the decent citizens either left of their own accord, or were forced out by the lawless breed, the wild ones who sought to further only their own ends, without thought for the future. He had seen these ghost towns for himself, riding the long, wide trails of Texas. Towns which had flourished briefly, springing up almost overnight, only to die an equally rapid death when the bandits and crooked lawmen rode in and tried to take over. Now the streets of these towns were empty but for the rolling balls of tumbleweed that drifted along on the dust-laden wind, drifting into the odd corners around the deserted buildings with their scattered windows and doors that hung gapingly open on broken hinges. Would the same thing happen to Fenton? The general indications were, unfortunately, that it would. Very soon, the rich veins of gold in the hills would be mined out, it would no longer be economic to work them and unless other reasons for staying in this town were found for the decent, wealthy people, it, too, would die an ignominious death like so many of the others.

He stepped out into the square and stood, letting the cool breeze blow on him. It was filled with the sweet smell of the distant hills and it felt good on his sunburnt face. He decided that it was still a little early to turn in and the surfeit of energy which his supper had provided was still working on him. He walked over to the edge of the square, along the main street, intending to go along to the edge of town and then walk back. A buckboard came rattling along the street, passed him at a steady trot. He noticed a grey-bearded man seated on the high step, then the other was gone and there was only the grey dust, kicked up by his passing, settling slowly in the air.

Walking slowly past the steepled church, he paused and lifted his gaze upward, beyond the tall spire, to where the quiet graves rested on the brow of the slope. He could see very little of the tremoring of starshine and after a few moments he walked on. Now that he was moving away from the area of saloons and gambling halls, the town was not too crowded. He saw an occasional figure on the far boardwalk and here and there a light showed in a window, but that was all. He felt glad of the silence and the stillness all around him, glad of the opportunity it gave him to think things out clearly in his mind.

So many events had happened, so swiftly, that it was a little difficult to be clear about any of them. He remembered what the doctor had said about Clem, when they had located has body in the alley. 'He'd been shot twice in the back and either bullet would have been enough to kill him. He had his gun in his hand, but it had been put there after he was dead.'

It was this that had twisted in Dave's stomach, turning a knife point in his mind, cutting through his brain until it was difficult for him to think straight any longer. This was his burden now. Clem had written to him, asking for his help. He had arrived too late to give that help. But not too late to avenge his partner, to hunt down his killer and see that he paid for it with his life. The burden had changed him. Now the restlessness in him was tempered with a vicious anger. He no longer had that vague air of carefree abandon which had marked his character until a little while before.

It was true that in the past he had been forced into situations when he had had to use a gun, to defend himself and to uphold law and order in some frontier hell town very much like this. But that had been different. There had been nothing really personal in it like this. Now this desire for revenge, for vengeance had become an obsession with him, giving him little rest. Maybe if he had been like some other men he would have gone out right away after Jed Sabine, called him out and shot him down. But his past rigid training demanded that he have decisive proof of the guilt of the man he killed. Besides, he was forced to admit there was also something else which had stopped him from doing this.

These past hours of thinking about this had abated the feeling of haste which had initially existed in his mind, the urge to get it over and done with as quickly as possible. At first, there had been a wild and almost overpowering anger burning in his mind, threatening to consume him to the exclusion of everything else. But now the urge to destroy Clem's killer, whoever he might be, in one stroke, was not enough. He knew that he wanted to let the other suffer before he died, that he had to make the other know who was pulling the trigger that sent him into eternity, and why he was doing it.

Suddenly, he realized that he was almost at the very edge of town. In front of him, in the gloom, the road wound out and away towards the far hills that lay humped on the skyline. There were only a handful of scattered huts lying in the dark stillness around him. He paused, a little uncertain now. The starlight laid a shimmering paleness over the undulating country around Fenton. It was light enough for him to see objects, but not light enough to be absolutely sure of what he saw.

Turning after a few moments, he began to walk back to the hotel. A dog came out of one of the dark-mouthed alleys, paused to eye him suspiciously and then walked over the street to the other side. He watched it for a moment, then went on. He was near the middle of the road when the shot rang out from one of the dark alleys that opened off to his right. From the edge of his vision he saw the brief spurt of orange, felt the wind of the bullet close to his cheek as it fled through the darkness near him. He dropped instantly to one knee, the gun in his hand as he turned. He sent a couple of shots whining up the alley, his face set tightly into a grim mask. There was the faint sound of the slugs ricocheting off the walls of the buildings on either side. A few moments later he heard a sharp yell and there was the sound of hooves on hard-baked earth. The rider shot forward, out of the gloomy shadow of the alley, coming on at a dead run, crouched low in the saddle. The sound of the horse, heading straight for him out of the darkness, was dull and heavy and seemed to grow in Dave's ears out of all proportion.

He knew instinctively that the other intended to run him down if he did not succeed in shooting him. He fired one more shot at random, aiming at the man leaning forward over the horse's neck. Then he got his legs under him, threw himself swiftly and instinctively to one side, rolling over and over in the dust in the direction of the boardwalk. The horse came at him, feet lashing at his head. He still retained his grip on his gun. Looming over him, he saw the dark shape of the man on the horse, the face hidden under the wide brim of the hat. A horseshoe struck him on the leg, sending a numbing shock of pain through him. Sucking air down into his lungs, he reached out with his right hand, felt the roughness of one of the wooden uprights, curled his fingers tightly around it and pulled himself with a desperate surge of strength over the high lip of the boardwalk. The wooden slats felt hard against his back and shoulders. He would have liked nothing better than to simply lie there and try to get his breath back into his aching lungs, but he knew he had to swing the rest of his body up into comparative safety. With a twist of his legs, he heaved himself on to the boardwalk, squirmed over on one side, fired a swift shot at the man looming over him. The bullet missed the other, but tore through the flesh of the horse's neck. With a shrill whinny of pain, the animal leapt high into the air, almost unseating the rider. Savagely the other fought to control the animal, but the horse was almost wild with the pain now. Wheeling it turned and galloped off into the darkness towards the edge of town. It was only with an effort that the man on its back succeeded in staying in the saddle.

Pushing himself up, Dave leaned his back against the upright, brushed the back of his hand over his grimy, sweat-stained face. The breeze felt icy cold on his body where the perspiration was beginning to congeal on his flesh.

Gripping the Colt tightly in his fist, he peered out into the darkness, straining his ears for any slight sound that would warn him of further danger in the long shadows, but apart from the creaking rustle of the wind through the slatted boards, there was nothing. The faint, tinny tinkle of a piano in one of the saloons drifted to him on the wind.

His whole body ached from the punishment it had taken, but gradually he managed to force the rapid beat of his heart into a slower, more normal, pace. The realization came to him that he had been far closer to death than he had previously thought. Whoever that man had been, he must have been in that alley when he had first walked out to the edge of town, must have been lying in wait, watching him, waiting for him to turn and walk back in the same direction.

He sat there for the best part of five minutes until he figured some of the strength had flowed back into his body, then heaved himself stiffly to his feet. Staggering a little, he made his way back into town, pausing frequently to hold on to the wooden uprights alongside the edge of the boardwalk as a sudden spasm of nausea went through him. His leg seemed bruised where the horse had kicked him, but it did not seem that anything had been seriously damaged and he was able to put his weight on it as he entered the square and walked over to the hotel.

The clerk behind the desk gave him a shocked look as he handed him the key of his room.

Dave forced a faint smile. 'Had a little accident,' he said quietly. 'My horse threw me when some *hombre* went by letting off his pistol into the air.'

'Of course, Mister Tremaine.' The other seemed to accept the explanation at once. His features remained quite smooth and bland. 'Would you like me to draw some water for a bath for you? It won't take above half an hour'

'Sure, thanks.' Dave nodded. 'Let me know when it's ready.'

'Of course, Mister Tremaine.' The other nodded, made a show of washing his hands and hurried off to search for the swamper.

The call came half an hour later and Dave went down stairs to the small room at the rear of the hotel. He found the water already drawn and in the large, wide basin, the steam rising in great clouds into the air. Slipping into the bath, he allowed the hot water to soak into his tired, bruised body, relaxing in the warmth. He lay there until the water began to cool, then dried himself briskly with a rough towel, went back up to his room. He took the precaution of pulling down the blinds before he lit the lamp on the small table.

Locking the door, he placed the key on the small table, sat on the edge of the bed and took off his boots. He had at least one dangerous enemy here in Fenton, he told himself. He did not know for sure who the other was, but he was a man who hated him or feared him so much that he had lain in wait in a dark alley, waiting his chance to shoot him down from cover. The fact that the other had also tried to trample him underfoot, was an indication of the intensity of the other's feelings. It was not any ordinary man intent on robbing him, he felt certain of that. He was equally sure it had not been Jed Sabine, or the crooked Sheriff of this town. The would-be killer had been a much slimmer man than Salmon and he also doubted the other's ability or courage to do such a thing.

He slid the long-barrelled Colt from its holster, stared down at the smooth shiny steel and the walnut butt. Spinning the chambers, he checked that he had loaded each of them after he had scared the other off, then he thrust the weapon back into its holster, placed it within easy reach on the table.

A faint anger swept through him, tightening the muscles of his chest and stomach. There was someone in Fenton who wanted him really and truly dead – not just so scared that he would run out of town, but dead,

Dave did not sleep as soundly as he had wished. The pain in his bruised leg kept intruding even into his unconscious mind, seeping into his dreams, and he tossed and turned on the bed for some hours before he found himself awake and cold. He lay for a long moment in the bed, staring up at the ceiling over his head. Deep inside him, he felt sure that some sound in the deep night stillness had wakened him and not the dull ache in his leg. The moon had risen now, although it was still dark and there was a pattern of moonlight on the floor of his room, a shifting pattern of light and shade as the curtains over the window – for he

had pulled aside the blinds when he had put out the light
– swayed lightly in the faint breeze.

Turning his head a little, he watched the play of light
and shadow on the floor near the bed, listening intently.
There was the faint sound of a horse from somewhere
outside and he had the feeling that it was very close by.
The livery stables were only a short distance across the
square, he recalled, and it could have come from there.
Then he noticed that the patch of light was changing
slowly. For several seconds he stared at it, trying to figure
out why it was altering. Carefully, moving his arm a little at
a time so as to make no sound, he reached out for the gun,
slid it smoothly from the oiled leather of the holster.
There was a dark shadow moving across the moonlight
where it cut a foot-wide swathe across the floor. He
propped himself up on one elbow, remembering that
there was a wide balcony running along the front of the
hotel, passing directly outside the window. It would be a
comparatively simple matter for a man to climb up on to
it and work his way along, or even step out from the
window of one of the other rooms fronting on to the
square.

The dark shape moved slowly, edging around the side
of the window. As yet, Dave was unable to see the other
except for the shadow he threw on the floor. He wondered
how long it would be before the other realized that this
shadow might be betraying him if his intended victim was
awake. Scarcely had the thought crossed his mind than the
shadow moved swiftly, all the way across to the other side
of the window.

Moving quickly, Dave slid back off the edge of the bed
furthest from the window, went down on his knees at the
side of it, and lined up the barrel of the Colt on the
window. He caught a glimpse of moonlight glinting off the
barrel of a revolver as the other angled it around through
the half-open window, hoping evidently to get a shot at the
man he imagined to be lying on the bed. Obviously the
other was familiar with the lay-out of the rooms in the

hotel. He had also known which room Dave had, which indicated that he had had access to the hotel register downstairs in the lobby.

A horse stomped outside, down in the street and this time Dave was certain that the sound had come from almost directly beneath his window. He was sure that it had not come from as far away as the livery stables.

He waited until he saw the hand which held the gun come into view, saw the man move around to make sure of his shot. The deep-rooted anger flared up once more in Dave's mind. This must be the same man who had tried to gun him down in the street a few hours before.

His gun steady in his hand, lined up on the target, he held his breath until it hurt in his lungs. What was the other doing now? he wondered. He heard at last a sigh come from the other. It was a sudden need for air that had betrayed what the other must have been feeling. The man seemed to know it, knew that the sound, faint as it was, might have awakened the man he imagined to be sleeping. The gun splashed fire into the dimness and the hard, loud sound of the shot reverberated around the room, deafening in the close confines of the place.

The Colt jerked in Dave's hand in virtually the same instant. It was almost impossible to get in a killing shot from that angle, but he heard the loud cry that went up from the other, saw the arm jerk away abruptly. Getting to his feet, he moved forward as quickly as he could, cursing a little under his breath as his injured leg threatened to go from under him. Grasping at the end of the bed, he hauled himself around, moved over to the window. There was a scuffling outside and he made out the scrape of a heavy body against the rough surface of the wall.

Throwing up the heavy window, he thrust his head out, throwing caution to the winds. He saw the dark shadow only briefly at the far end of the balcony. Lifting the Colt, he aimed a shot at the other, then let the pressure of his finger off the trigger. The other was gone, around the side of the building, swinging himself lightly out from the balcony. A moment later, he heard the sound of a horse down below, strained forward in an attempt to pick out the rider, but the other kept well into the side of the street so that the overhang prevented Dave from seeing him.

There came a loud and persistent knocking at the door and a voice yelled something from the corridor outside. Holstering the gun, Dave went across the room and unlocked the door. A dishevelled clerk stood there, a shot-gun in his hand and a candle in the other.

'Are you all right, Mister Tremaine? I heard some shooting.'

'Some critter tried to kill me,' Dave said slowly. 'He was on the balcony outside, tried to shoot in through the window.'

'But I don't understand. Do you know who it was? Maybe if I got the sheriff he could get a posse together and go after him.'

Dave shook his head slowly. 'He's got too good a start now. Besides, I only caught a vague glimpse of him, it was too dark for me to see who he was. It could have been almost anyone.'

'What do you intend to do?' asked the other tautly. There was a faint tremor in his voice and his eyes protruded from their sockets as he stared past Dave into the room.

'Somehow, I don't figure he'll try again during the night. I winged him with a slug in the arm.'

'Then I'll wish you good night.' The other moved off along the corridor, evidently glad to be away and equally glad that there was not going to be a scandal involving the hotel.

Relocking the door, Dave went back to the window, peered down into the street. As far as he could see in either direction, it was deserted. Not a soul was moving. The moon, near full, threw a web of silver over the sleeping town, touching the walls of the buildings with its pale, cold light. The alleys were dark, open mouths that looked out on to the main street where the dust gleamed faintly.

Closing the window, he pulled the shutters across, went back to the bed and stretched himself out on it, pulling the single blanket over him. The air was still warm inside the room and he lay on his back for a while turning things over in his mind, his forehead knit in thought. The answer lay at the back of his mind, kept pushing its way forward, but it was one he did not like, one he did not want to have to act upon.

He tried to make his thoughts think on Virginia Corrie, remembering the grace and quiet beauty of her, the way her eyes looked at him clearly and softly, the gentle curve of her lips and the even white teeth when she smiled. But try as he would, his thoughts of her kept slipping away and his mind kept coming back to the one thing.

There was only one man who could have been responsible for these two treacherous attempts on his life; the only man who feared him so much that he wanted him dead and did not care how he killed him – Luke Corrie, Virginia's brother.

FIVE

VENGEANCE TRAIL

At times during the morning, Dave would think about the man called Luke Corrie, trying to figure out what sort of a man he was, whether he had been so completely corrupted by Sabine that he would be irredeemable, or whether he was only acting out of fear for his own skin, sincerely believing that Dave was gunning for him, knowing that he did not have a chance in hell of outdrawing the man who had shot down Cantry, Sabine's top gunman, in the Broken Lance saloon.

Dave liked to think that it was the latter reason which had prompted the other to try to kill him in the ways he had. It had come as a strange shock to him, but reason and commonsense told him that he could not possibly be wrong, that it was Virginia's brother who was trying to dry-gulch him. The big question was: could he possibly get the other and make him see reason before one or both of them were killed?

The rocks that lined this stretch of the trail stood out tall and clean in the flooding sunlight but in the early morning, the floor of the canyon was still in deep shadow almost the whole of the way across. He could pick out the shrill cries of the birds in the stunted trees that grew in the distance and the soft soughing of the wind in the branches. He splashed over a narrow stream and up into a broad clearing. The town of Fenton had still been slumbering fitfully when he had eaten his breakfast and ridden out, taking the trail east, back towards the Corrie spread.

He rested the sorrel in the clearing for ten minutes, then continued along the trail, every sense alert, watchful for impending trouble. He could not be certain that his departure had not been seen and it was possible he was being trailed, even now. He paused at every vantage point and watched his back trail, but for almost an hour, there had been no sign of the tell-tale dust that would have given away to him the presence of some other rider.

Dave did not press his mount. The sorrel knew its own pace and stuck to it, but they made good progress. Gradually, the character of the land around him began to change. It grew more rocky, more open, the trail winding in and out of tall boulders that stood high on the skyline. Here, with the heat increasing in intensity, he found that he could see further along the trail behind him and also across the country that lay on either side of him, but in also meant that he could be seen for a much greater distance.

This was the sparsely inhabited country that lay between the lush cattle spreads close to the borders of Fenton, and the more outlying ranches between the river and the desert. Putting his mount to the upgrade, he pursued the trail for almost a mile before it levelled out into a wide plateau. Pressing the sorrel well into the side of the trail, he twisted in the saddle and peered into the shimmering heat haze behind him, eyes narrowed against the sickening glare. At first, he could see nothing, the trail still apparently deserted. Then, off in the distance, smaller than a man's hand, he saw the trail smoke and knew that there was a rider, or a bunch of riders, spurring their mounts swiftly along the trail he had taken.

Whoever it was on his trail he did not wish to argue the point with them at that particular time. Touching spurs to the sorrel's flanks, he sent it bounding forward along the rock-strewn slope. This was difficult country for a horse to navigate, but the sorrel seemed to sense that he was in a hurry and laid its ears well back, the wind streaming past them as they raced for the far side of the plateau. Thrusting aside the slender branches of the oak saplings that overgrew on to the trail from both sides, ignoring the pain as they sometimes slashed back, striking him savagely across the face and shoulders, he succeeded in keeping himself in the saddle, holding on to the reins tightly with both hands, his body bent low over the horse's neck. He estimated that he still had close on three miles of a lead over the men behind him and felt sure that if he could maintain this lead while he got down into the level valley that lay beyond the hills, the sorrel would easily outrun any other horse. The sorrel was tired, he could feel that in the way it sometimes stumbled as they rode over a partic-ularly treacherous and rough patch and its feet were evidently sore from the white alkali of the stretch of desert they had crossed before climbing the upgrade into the hills, but it was a thoroughbred and such an animal could always get that little extra bit of speed, of endurance from itself if pushed.

It was certainly being pushed now. The spurs were raking at times across its flanks and it must have got the idea that this was really serious business it was engaged upon for it took the bit between its teeth, its tail came up and it went down at breakneck speed, almost coming right down on to its nose as the downgrade steepened sharply. Dave jerked his legs straight against the stirrups, holding himself rigid in the saddle to help the animal keep its feet on the shifting shale underfoot.

They came down from the hills and hit the smoother ground of the valley less than twenty minutes later, the horse leaping forward in a long series of bounding, hurdling strides. Dave gave a quick glance behind him, but he could see no sign of any pursuit along the hill trail that stretched up behind him for close on two miles to the narrow pass at the top. Evidently the others were not wishing to take such risks as he had along that dangerous stretch of the trail.

He found no difficulty here in picking his way through the brush and cacti that grew in profusion and a little further on, he swung the sorrel off the trail. There was a tall stand of young pines in the distance and he made for it. Ten minutes later he was hidden by a tangle of vines and catsclaw which grew around the trunks of the trees. The sorrel became hipshot almost at once, nostrils flaring, chest heaving as it drew air deeply into his lungs. Less than a minute later the bunch of men appeared in the near distance and Dave realized that they had tricked him, they had not taken the trail over the hills, but had swung around them by what may have been a shorter, and certainly an easier trail.

They appeared to be checking the ground at intervals and he gently eased the Colt from its holster as he watched them move towards the point where he had moved away from the trail. If they discovered what he had done and came riding towards his hiding place, he was determined to sell his life dearly. They drew level with the place where he had turned off, kept right on, moving in a tight bunch. He counted seven of them, recognized the man who rode in the lead. It was almost impossible to mistake the portly figure of Sheriff Ben Salmon. A grim smile played on his lips for a moment as he watched them ride by, sending up a cloud of white dust to mark their trail. The lawman had certainly wasted no time in riding out after him. Obviously Salmon felt brave now that he had men riding with him.

Waiting until the posse had moved on, out of sight, he rolled himself a smoke, giving the sorrel a chance to get back its wind. It came to him that the logical place for that posse to be heading would be the Corrie ranch, his own destination. They would know, of course, that he had spent one night there and it seemed the only place where he could return to after leaving town, unless he had been fool enough to ride alone into Sabine's camp.

Not until he finished his smoke did he ride out of the

shelter of the grove, out on to the trail once more. There was the sharp, acrid smell of dust still lingering in the air but no sign of the posse. He kept off the main trail and selected a narrow ravine, putting the horse down into it, the high rocky walls hiding him from view. Halfway along the ravine they encountered a small pool of water and he let the animal drink, lying flat on his own stomach and drinking his fill. When he had finished he took off his hat, filled it with water and poured it over his head.

Continuing to thread their way along the ravine, they worked their way around huge boulders which had, at some past age, been moved into the ravine, possibly by the action of water when a river had once worked its way along this narrow rift in the earth. At times, the boulders were so huge that they almost filled all of the space on the floor of the ravine and he was forced to dismount and lead the horse around them.

Pausing for a while after he reached the end of the ravine, he gazed cautiously about him. He was not exactly sure of what he was going to do now, but he had the faint notion that Virginia Corrie and her father might help him, although what they could do in the face of the pressure that Sabine could bring to bear against him, he did not know.

Whatever he did, he would have to make sure that the posse was no longer at the ranch. Salmon would probably insist on searching the place when he got there, confident that Dave was hiding some place on the land. Not until he had satisfied himself that this was not the case would he start to backtrack in the hope of finding him somewhere along the trail. He could imagine what the lawman's thoughts would be when he discovered that Dave had somehow given him the slip somewhere along the trail. The other must have been so certain that he had him cold.

It was almost noon and the sun was beating down with a relentless fierceness when he finally rode through the trees on top of the low hill which overlooked the Corrie ranch. Reining up, he sat tall in the saddle, peering down through the thin fringe of trees. He could make out the ranch house down below him, the wide stretch of the courtyard in front of the building. There was a solitary horse in the corral, but several tied to the rail in front of the porch. Even as he watched, a small group of men came out of the house and made their way over to the low-roofed bunk-house. Dave nodded to himself. The Sheriff and his posse were still there, searching the place as he had suspected they would.

Once they discovered nothing they would realize they had been tricked, that they had missed him somewhere along the trail. From where he was, he could see everything that went on down there and dismounting, he moved to the edge of the grove, sat down on a small boulder, and built himself a smoke. He was quite content to wait until Salmon was through with his abortive search and had gone before riding down there.

The search carried out by the posse was thorough and painstaking. They missed nothing. It was almost three-quarters of an hour before Salmon went back into the house; came out five minutes later and called his men together, swinging himself up into the saddle. His back against the trunk of one of the trees, Dave watched the men ride out with the Sheriff in the lead, cutting back on to the trail which led west towards Fenton. He gave them time to get well away, then cut back into the trees, bent to tighten the cinch under the sorrel's belly and climbed into the saddle.

His leg still ached where the horse had kicked him the day before and he gritted his teeth as a sharp spasm of pain lanced through it with every movement he made. Slowly he rode down the hill, across the plank bridge and into the courtyard. He was still a few yards from the house when the door opened and Virginia Corrie stepped out on to the porch, shading her eyes against the sun. Stepping down, she ran across to him, caught at the reins.

'Sheriff Salmon was here looking for you a little while ago, Dave,' she said, a trifle breathlessly.

'I know.' He smiled a little as he got down, stood beside her. 'I was up there on top of the hill watching him as he searched the place. I'm real sorry that this had to happen and involve you, Virginia, but that's just how things panned out, I'm afraid.'

'You don't have to apologize to us, Dave. But why are they looking for you?'

'I'm not sure. There was some shooting yesterday in the saloon there. A man called Cantry, one of Sabine's top gunmen, called me out. I had to kill him. Guess that Salmon wanted to make sure I was under lock and key until Sabine decided what to do with me.'

'But why did he come here?' she asked, walking beside him, back to the house.

'I reckon it was because somehow word got into Fenton that we met on the trail when I rode into this territory and I spent the night here with your father and yourself. Maybe they figured that this was the first place I'd head for when 1 rode out of town this mornin'.'

'I'm glad you did come back here,' she said softly. 'I wondered what might have happened to you in Fenton.'

'There's something that I think you ought to know before we go any further, something I want to talk over with you before I see your father.'

'What is it, Dave?' The seriousness of his face and voice had not been lost on her and her own tone was equally sober.

'Yesterday, a man tried to kill me, not once, but twice. He first made a try by bushwhacking me in the street, tried to ride me down with his horse when he couldn't kill me with a bullet. Then he made another attempt while I was in bed in the hotel, worked his way along the balcony outside my room and fired a shot through the window.'

He saw the worried look on her face, knew, however, that she had not made even a guess at the truth.

'But why should anyone do that, unless—' She broke

off as a thought struck her. 'Unless he was your friend's killer.'

Very slowly, Dave shook his head. 'I'm pretty sure he wasn't Clem's murderer. He wanted to kill me for a somewhat different reason.' He paused, bit his lower lip, then went on: 'It ain't easy for me to say this, Virginia, and I've got to admit that I never even saw this man's face, but I'm fairly certain it was your brother.'

'Luke!' He saw the expression of shocked horror written on her features. 'But that can't be true. Why would he want to kill you?'

'I think it's because he believes he killed Clem and he's sure that I'm gunnin' for him. He maybe knows he wouldn't stand a chance against me in an even fight and before running the risk of me catchin' him, he tried to kill me like that.'

'And do you think that he killed your friend?' There was a tremor in the girl's voice as she somehow got the words out.

'No, I'm sure he didn't. He was arrested for the killing but I know he didn't do it.'

'I'm glad.' The relief in her tone was distinctly audible. 'But what are you going to do?'

Dave sighed. 'I only wish I knew. Somehow, I have to get to him before he does kill me and make him see that I don't believe he's Clem's murderer.'

'How can you do that if he still works for Sabine?' countered the girl. They reached the house and stepped inside. Lex Corrie was in the parlour. He glanced up quickly as they came in, showed little surprise when he saw Dave.

'I figured you might be along, Tremaine,' he said quietly. 'When Salmon rode in and insisted on searching the place, I guessed he must have had a good reason for thinkin' you were hidin' here. What happened?'

'Dave has something to say, Dad,' said Virginia slowly. She walked over and stood beside her father, one hand on his shoulder. 'I think you ought to listen. And don't get angry. It concerns Luke.'

Dave saw the other's mouth tighten at the mention of his son's name, saw the faint lift of his shoulders as he sat more stiffly in his chair. The knuckles of his fingers whitened a little in the hands that grasped the sides of the chair. Then he said tightly: 'You bring me news of my son, Tremaine. What is it you have to say? I think you know how I feel about Luke, since he threw in his lot with that crook and killer, Jed Sabine.'

'I know how you feel,' Dave said quietly. He lowered himself into the chair opposite the other. 'But there are several things you ought to know before you pass judgement on him. Believe me, at this moment, I have more cause to hate him than you have. He twice tried to kill me last night.'

A tiny muscle twitched high in the older man's cheek. For a moment he remained silent as if not trusting himself to speak. Then he said tautly: 'Frankly, that does not surprise me, Tremaine, for the reports I have received of him. He has lowered himself to the level of the coyotes he rides with.'

'Your son was arrested a few weeks ago, charged with the murder of Clem Fordyce, the man I came to see. He was put in jail by Ben Salmon and then released the next day when Sabine rode into town with a bunch of his men.'

A hard, fixed smile appeared on Corrie's lips. It was almost as if it had been painted on. 'That too, comes as no surprise to me,' he said stiffly, through lips that scarcely seemed to move.

'I'm afraid it isn't quite what you think,' Dave went on quietly. 'When I rode into town, nobody would tell me anythin' about the shootin'. Seems they were scared of Sabine and his crew. But Doc Keller seemed sure that your son was far too drunk to have shot anyone on that particular night and he believes, just as I do, that he was framed for this killin'. I think, too, that Sabine framed him so that he would have an even tighter hold over him than he did before.'

'And do you know what hold he had originally on Luke?'

'Yes. Seems he got into a crooked poker game with some gambler. When the game finished, he found himself owing the gambler nearly two thousand dollars. Naturally, he couldn't pay that sort of money, but Sabine paid it for him, keeping his IOUs as security. I think Luke had no choice but to go to work for Sabine. Jed doesn't seem to me to be the sort of man who would let anyone who owed him two thousand dollars off the hook once he had him in his power.'

Lex Corrie sat forward in his chair, staring straight in front of him, a strangely blank expression on his face. Then he finally stirred himself and there was a deep wrath stirring at the back of his eyes. 'If what you tell me is true, then I have a score to settle with Sabine that goes beyond his attempts to take away this ranch from me. He's stolen my son and that means far more to me than the house, land and cattle.'

'I'm sure it does,' Dave said gently. 'But it won't help to let your anger get control over you. If you try to fight Sabine single-handed, you would never have a chance. We need help to finish Sabine.'

Corrie sat slumped a little in his chair. 'Where would we get help like that?' he asked in a dull, flat tone. 'You know as well as I do that none of the other ranchers will band together to fight him. I tried to get them to see the sense of that some time ago. They're all scared for their own skins. Not that you can blame them, I reckon, when you think of hired gunslingers such as Cantry that Sabine has on his payroll.'

'Like Sabine *had* on his payroll,' Dave corrected.

Corrie stared across at him in sudden surprise. 'You mean that Cantry is dead?' he asked incredulously.

'That's right.' Dave gave a quick nod. 'He called me out in the saloon. Admitted that Sabine had paid him to kill me.'

'And you outdrew and outshot Cantry?' Corrie looked at Dave as if he could scarcely believe his ears.

'It was either him or me,' Dave said modestly. 'I guess

he wasn't quite as good as he figured he was.'

'If I know Sabine, he won't be long in fetchin' in some other gunslinger. You're pushin' him mighty hard. He won't like that.'

'Right now, I'm worried about Luke. Sabine must've told him that I'm in the territory and he won't have wasted any time tellin' him why I'm here. Luke figures that he has to kill me before I drop him.'

'I take your point, son,' nodded the other. 'It ain't an easy position to be in. But you say that he wasn't around town when you left this mornin'.'

'Never saw him. I hit him in the arm last night with a slug. Could be that Doc Keller knows where he's headed. Reckon Keller is the only man he could go to if he wanted his arm fixed.' Dave noticed the look on the girl's face and went on hastily. 'It weren't no bad wound, Virginia. Lucky for me I did get him there or he may have tried again.'

'You did the only thing you could Dave,' Virginia Corrie said in a low voice. 'I guess that all we can do is apologize for my brother. If there is anything that we can do to help, you have only to ask.'

'I'll have another try at gettin' the ranchers around here to band together against Sabine. Mebbe once they know that his ace gunslinger, Cantry, is dead, they may think again and throw in their lot with us.' Corrie's face was tight. 'But if they won't listen, even then, what can we do? Sabine has the whip hand and he knows it.'

Dave said grimly: 'What about the townsfolk? Do you reckon any of them will stand against Sabine and his crew?'

Corrie's forehead wrinkled in sudden thought. 'Hard to say what they'd do. From what I've seen of 'em, I don't reckon there's one who has the guts to stand up to him. Can't blame 'em, I guess. I've been around long enough to know what happens when a cattle crew like Sabine's braces a trail town. They'll burn every goddamned building to the ground.'

Flashpoint

'I know their breed,' Dave said coolly. 'Just so long as there's a big enough bunch of 'em, they're pretty brave.' He shrugged his shoulders. 'One thing I would like to know. Whether what I've told you about Luke has changed your mind at all.'

Corrie glanced up sharply. There was an odd expression on his face. 'Now why do you ask that?' he inquired.

'Because unless I miss my guess, Sabine is soon goin' to become kill-crazy and he may decide that Luke is more of a liability to him than an asset. After all, he's tried twice to kill me, and each time he's failed. Sabine isn't goin' to give him many more chances and sooner or later, Luke is goin' to meet up with somebody in town who isn't scared to talk and he may start puttin' some of the answers he gets together and comin' up with the idea that maybe he didn't kill Clem after all, that he's been framed for this murder.'

'From what you say, I'm convinced I acted wrongly,' said the other slowly. 'Maybe Luke was wrong in playin' poker with that crooked gambler, but goddamn, I guess I did the same myself in my young days.' His voice dropped a little, became deadly serious. 'I want him back, Dave. I want him back here alive, where he belongs.'

'That's what I was hopin' you'd say'

'But how are you goin' to convince him that you're not aimin' to kill him?' The lines around the corners of the other's eyes and mouth deepened just a shade. 'If he's ridin' with Sabine's bunch, it won't be easy to get through to him.'

'Reckon you can leave that problem with me.' Dave got to his feet, winced a little as his injured leg gave slightly under his weight. He saw the immediate look of concern on Virginia's face as she stepped forward towards him.

'Dave, you're hurt!'

'Nothing much. Just a kick I got from Luke's horse. No bones broken.'

'I'll boil some water and bathe it for you.' She turned towards the kitchen door, paused as Dave said quickly: 'No time for that, Virginia. I guess this can wait. When Salmon and his posse find no trace of me back yonder in the hills, I figure they may come back here, guessin' that I've outsmarted them.'

'Take care, Dave,' she said softly as he moved towards the porch door. 'One man doesn't have much of a chance against a bunch of hired killers like those Jed Sabine has gathered around him. Even though you outdrew Cantry, it won't take Sabine long to bring in some other fast gun to make his play for you.'

'I'll remember that, Virginia' He paused for a moment, then stepped out into the courtyard, into the white dust and the hot sunlight.

SIX

DANGER TRAIL

With the high, bright stars still showing against the clear sky of early dawn, Dave Tremaine was still riding. He had swung around in a vast semi-circle after leaving the Corrie ranch, heading north. On the way he had ridden silently past several small line camps, but had stopped at none of them, just riding quietly by in the darkness, close enough to be reasonably certain that they were Sabine's men who occupied them, then pushing on the pace.

Now he stopped, reining up his mount. The fence had been newly built. The posts were of fresh-cut pine oak and it was laid out, arrow straight along the banks of the stream that ran through the grass country, its banks eroded in places. Dave reckoned that this fence marked the boundary of what had once been Roxanna's spread until Sabine had forced her out.

Easing his mount along the fence, he came to a spot where a group of willows grew up out of the soft earth by the stream. Whoever had hammered the wire home had made a slipshod job of it here, for the nails had torn loose of the trunks of the trees and the wire was trailing in the swirling water. He put his mount through the gap, rode up the steep slope on the far side. Entering a deep valley that cut through two rough shoulders of ground, he rode more carefully now, not expecting trouble out here but alert for it. Yet when it came, it was totally unexpected.

The rifle shot came from behind him, the bullet chewing a slice of dirt from the rocky wall to his right. He made a quick, instinctive slide to the left in the saddle, reached down for his gun, froze as the mocking voice called: 'You'll be seconds late, Tremaine, but if you want to give me the excuse for killin' you, then go right ahead.'

Dave stiffened abruptly. It was a voice he recognized. One of the men who had been in the Broken Lance when he had outshot Cantry. He felt a momentary anger flare within him. The other must have seen him across the stream, had probably been in the trees, waiting.

Slowly, he lifted his hands, not turning his head. The man behind him said softly: 'Now that's better, ain't it, Luke?'

There was the sound of booted feet scrabbling on the rocks, then a short, squat shape edged around into the line of Dave's vision. He had not been mistaken. The Winchester was laid directly on him, the man's finger hard on the trigger.

'Careful, Shorty. He's a real mean one.' Another man came into view on Dave's other side.

Dave glanced at him, gave out a level stare. 'You Luke Corrie?' he asked brusquely.

'That's right first time,' grinned the other. He jumped down into the floor of the valley a couple of yards in front of the other, hands swinging close to the guns in their holsters. 'I figgered I'd meet up with you sooner or later if I only waited long enough.'

'Mind if I put my hands down now?' Deliberately Dave turned to the other man. 'Gets a mite tirin' holdin' them up like this.'

'OK. But make the first wrong move and it'll give me

the greatest pleasure to put a slug between your eyes.'

'No you won't, Shorty!' snapped Corrie harshly. 'I want him. I've got to be sure he's dead, to keep him off my back. You know why you've got to die, here and now, Tremaine, don't you?'

Slowly, every movement deliberate, Dave leaned forward and rested his arms on the saddlehorn, looking directly at the other. 'I know why you figure you have to kill me, Luke,' he said quietly. 'Because you think you killed my pardner, Clem Fordyce.'

'What d'you mean, *think* I killed him?' demanded the other roughly. There was a new note in his voice, the beginnings of doubt. Dave knew he had to play on these doubts, build them up into something more.

He shook his head slowly. 'You didn't kill Fordyce, Luke. I know for a fact that you were in no condition to kill anybody that night. Only Sabine wants you to think you did. That way he's got a real tight hold over you. He can make you jump like a branded steer any time he wants to. He can send you out to kill me, just by makin' you so damn scared that I'm gunnin' for you.'

'Don't listen to him, kid,' said the other man harshly. 'He's only sayin' this because he knows we've got the drop on him this time. He'll say anythin' to save his own neck.' There was an ominous click as the other forced another bullet into the breech. 'Let's finish this now. You know what Sabine's orders were.'

'No. If he's lyin' we can always take that into account when we kill him. But I want to hear what he's got to say.'

'Sabine ain't goin' to like this when he hears.'

'You figurin' on tellin' him?' asked the other harshly.

'Mebbe. If you ain't goin' to kill him, then I am.' The Winchester lifted, the barrel laid on Dave's chest.

'Seems to me you're mighty anxious to shoot me down in cold blood so as to stop me talkin',' Dave said in a soft, guarded way. 'Maybe you're the killer who shot Fordyce in the back and then fired a couple of shots from Luke's weapon before leaving him, dead drunk in the alley near Fordyce's body?'

'Why you—'

'Hold it right there, Shorty!' There was a Colt in Luke's hand now and it was pointed at the other man. 'What this *hombre* is sayin' makes sense. I was so drunk that night that I don't remember anythin' that happened. I've only got the word of Sabine and the others. Now put that Winchester down.'

'Like hell I will,' roared the other. Out of the corner of his eye, Dave saw the squat man swing his weapon, loose off a single shot. The bullet caught Luke Corrie in the shoulder, spun him round, the Colt falling from his nerveless fingers.

Before Shorty could turn and bring the weapon to bear again, Dave had thrown himself out of the saddle, kicking off with a powerful heave of his legs. His arms and shoulders hit Shorty square in the chest, sending him hurtling backwards on the hard ground, the Winchester flying from his grasp.

Dave kneed his man savagely as they fell on to the ground and there was a bleating agony in Shorty's choked cry. He doubled forward, then swung his fist, driving it out in front of him like a piston. Dave, turning his head a little as he saw it coming, took most of the vicious blow on his shoulder but even so, the other's fist skidded on the flesh at the side of his neck, shaking him up. Lights flashed in front of his eyes and he fell to one side, gasping for air.

Savagely, Shorty rolled over. There was sweat on his face and his lips were still twisted up into a grimace of pain, but he seemed to have fought down most of the sickness that had come surging up from that first savage blow of the knee in the stomach. Another swinging blow curved around to the back of Dave's head, the knotted fist hammering at his skull.

Shorty Frye took immediate advantage of his position. Struggling to his feet his boot lashed out, caught Dave on the thigh, hurling him back, down the slope, his body bouncing on to the rocks below, all of the wind knocked out of him by the impact of the fall. Through blurred vision, he saw Frye leaping down on top of him, arms spread wide, but with his knees close together, held so that they would crash down with all of his weight behind them on Dave's stomach, pinning him to the ground. There was only a split second in which to act and Dave acted instinctively.

One leg still bent where he had landed on the rough earth, he thrust off sharply with it, rolling his body over in a despairing movement. Shorty came down on his knees in the dirt, uttered a wild, high-pitched yell of agony, fell forward, floundering with his arms clutching at Dave as he rolled free. The impact of landing on his bent knees had hurt the other badly, but he was still full of fight, still potentially dangerous. Even as Dave struggled to come upright, a fist closed around his left ankle, hung on grimly with a grip that he was unable to shake off. Shorty held on to his man, trying to pull him down. His face was a terrible thing in the dawn light, lips pulled back from the broken, stained teeth, eyes bulging from their sockets like those of a madman. He was breathing heavily in stuttering gasps through his open mouth, throat muscles working, his adam's apple bobbing up and down in his bull-like neck.

Driving forward with his shoulder, bringing it sharply into the pit of Dave's stomach, he sent him staggering back against the rock wall of the canyon, the breath whooshing from Dave's lungs. For a moment, darkness hovered in front of his eyes and he felt the strength drain from him. Shorty backed off a couple of paces. When he came in again, there was the faint flicker of light on the blade of the knife he held in his right hand, holding it straight out in front of him, the point aimed at Dave's throat.

For a moment they circled each other warily. Dave kept his eyes fixed on the knife in the other's hand, watching

for the first move. It came a second later, thrusting and
slashing forward in a single sweeping movement. He
skipped back, ran the tip of his tongue around his dry
lips. There was no doubt that this man knew how to
handle a knife. He must have used one on many occasions in bar-room brawls and the like.

Grinning viciously, Shorty Frye came in again, grunting
a little, eyes fixed on Dave's face. 'Sabine's sent for a fast
gun to finish you once and for all, Tremaine,' he hissed
through his teeth. 'But I'm reckonin' he won't need him
now.'

Dave's answer to that was to lunge forward, a tightly-
bunched fist driving ahead of him, ducking under the
knife hand. The move took Frye by surprise. He had been
expecting Dave to continue moving back in the face of the
knife threat. The blow caught Shorty on the side of the
head, knocking him backwards, but not off balance. He
recovered, came in again, moved forward in a series of
lunges, circling around to Dave's right all the time. Too
late the other realized the reason for this. Stepping back
instinctively as the other slashed at his face with the knife,
his foot caught the loose boulder immediately behind
him, his leg going from under him, pitching him on to his
back.

Shorty Frye leapt in at once, striking down with the
knife at Dave's throat. Swiftly, knowing it was his only
hope, Dave caught the other's wrist, forcing it back with
all the strength he could muster. Still the knife edged
slowly towards his throat as the other threw all of his
weight into the battle. There was a roaring in Dave's ears
like the thunderous clamour of a waterfall inside his
skull. He jerked his head to one side suddenly, swinging
with his arms, bringing up his leg at the same time. For a
moment the other teetered helplessly, then slithered to
one side. Acting almost without conscious thought, Dave
kicked up with his right leg, caught the other man in the
middle of the stomach, hurling him through the air and
back against the rocks where he fell in a twisted heap.

Dave lay flat on the ground for some moments, breathing deeply, waiting for his head to clear and the pounding inside his skull to lessen. Then he struggled to his feet, moved cautiously towards the still figure on the ground, alert for a trick, bent carefully and rolled the man over. Unseeing eyes stared up at the brightening dawn sky. There was blood on the man's chest and the hilt of the knife, still clutched tenaciously in the dead fingers, protruded from his body, where it had been driven deeply into his heart as he had fallen on it.

Rubbing the sweat from his face, wincing from the bruises along his ribs, he went over to where Luke Corrie had managed to push himself up on to his hands and knees, head swinging loosely between his arms.

'Just sit back there and let me take a look at that shoulder of yours,' he said quietly.

Blood had soaked into the other's shirt. The bullet had gone in high up on the right side. It had bled a lot and there was the chance he had been lung-shot. If he was to live, he would have to be got to a doctor as soon as possible.

'Reckon you can stay in the saddle until we get to Fenton?' Dave asked.

'I guess so,' gritted the other through tightly-clenched teeth. 'How bad is it? Is it the big one, Tremaine?'

'I don't reckon so. May have nicked the lung though and you've lost a lot of blood. Now don't try to talk. I'll pad it up to help staunch the blood, then get you into the saddle.' Tearing several strips of cloth from his shirt, he packed them tightly against the wound, binding it as well as he could.

'Your bronc down near the stream?' he asked at last.

The other nodded dully, his eyes glazed as the pain began to show through on his face.

Dave made his way slowly back to the stream, whistled up the other's horse, caught at the bridle and led it back to where Luke sat with his shoulders against the rocks. The other moaned deep in his throat as Dave hoisted him limply into the saddle. For a moment he thought the other would never make it. There seemed to be no strength left in his body. He swayed and drooped in the saddle, leaning forward over the horse's neck. Swinging up into his own saddle, Dave caught the other's reins and led the horse slowly back, across the stream, through the gap in the fence, heading south across the open range-land towards Fenton.

In the back room of Doc Keller's place, Dave Tremaine sat on the edge of the long, low bunk and waited for Luke Corrie to regain consciousness. As he watched the other, he thought of this man who had been so close to death by the time he had managed to get him into Fenton, and of other men who were now dead. Clem Fordyce, Cantry the gunslick, Shorty Frye, whose body still lay out there on the edge of Roxanna's original spread. In each case it had taken nothing more than a tiny piece of speeding lead to do all of this, to kill a man or bring him to the point of death. Or the slender piece of steel that was a bowie knife. Men were, when one came to look at things objectively, very fragile things, easily destroyed.

'He'll be conscious in a little while,' Doc Keller said. He bent and felt the other's pulse. 'In a way, I'm glad it turned out this way. He ain't really bad like those others who ride with Sabine. Just too easily led.'

'Sure,' Dave nodded. He stared down at the man on the bunk, the white of the bandages around his upper chest standing out starkly against the tanned skin of the neck. He saw the first, faint stirrings of consciousness return to Luke Corrie. The fluttering of the eyelids, the tiny twitch-ing muscle at the side of the mouth. Then the other's eyes open and the blankness of incomprehension flickered into a look of conscious recognition.

'Tremaine.' The word was little more than a harsh, husky whisper, like dry balls of tumbleweed rasping along a dusty street.

'I'm here,' said Dave quietly. 'Now just lie still and take things easy. You're goin' to be all right. Doc got the slug out of your shoulder. All you need now is rest and quiet.'

'You think Sabine will let me live after this? I know too much about him, Tremaine. A whole heap too much.'

'Easy does it,' said Keller. 'You're safe here.'

The other relaxed a little. Then he went on again, his voice growing a little stronger, as if urgency was giving him added strength. 'Sabine's sent for a top gunman, Tremaine, Kid Moran. He's due in on the stage today or tomorrow. Sabine's payin' him five hundred dollars to kill you. Any way he likes.'

'That so?' Sombreness was a cloak on Tremaine and the sudden harshness pulled his face into deep craggy lines. 'Thanks for givin' me fair warnin'.' Quite suddenly, he relaxed, grinned down at the other. 'At least it shows we've forced Sabine's hand and got him on the run.'

'Don't think cheap of men like Kid Moran,' warned the other. He half propped himself up on one elbow. 'Cantry was fast, I'll admit, but Moran is a rattler. He's lightnin' fast.'

'I'll watch him if he does ride in,' Dave said. He got off the edge of the bunk in one single, lithe movement at a sudden knocking on the door. Doc Keller went over, opened it a couple of inches, peering out, then opened it all the way. Roxanna hurried in, looked about her for a moment, then ran to the bunk and went down on one knee beside it.

'Luke! Oh Luke!'

Corrie grinned weakly at her. 'I'm all right, Roxy,' he said harshly. 'Just a slug in the shoulder. Doc got it out for me. Reckons I'll be on my feet in a week or so.'

The girl looked inquiringly around at Keller and the old man nodded in affirmation.

'There was talk at the saloon that Tremaine had brought you in dead,' she said thinly. She laid a hard glance on Dave, her look silently accusing.

'It weren't Dave,' Luke said quietly. 'He saved my life. Shorty Frye shot me down after we'd jumped Dave on that stretch that used to be your property.'

Roxanna was silent for a few moments, then got to her feet and walked over to Dave. 'I'm sorry, Mr Tremaine,' she said, placing a hand on his arm. 'I guess I'm all mixed up right now. But I knew that Luke here was gunning for you and when they said that—'

'I understand, Roxanna.' Dave glanced down at the wounded man. 'Can you look after him with Doe here? It's just possible there might be trouble when Sabine finds out about this.'

'Don't worry, if Sabine and his gunmen come here they'll get more than they bargained for.' There was a lot of determination in the set of her chin. Dave reckoned that she could give a good account of herself if it came to a showdown.

When the stage hauled up in front of the depot at three o'clock that afternoon, Jed Sabine and his foreman were there to meet it. Sabine gave each of the passengers a brush with his gaze as they stepped down, then touched Forrest's arm. 'There's our man,' he said shortly, nodding towards the character who stepped down last from the stage.

The man who stood looking about him was in his early thirties. A short, spare man, thin almost to the point of gauntness, but with a snake-like wiriness about him. He wore a gunbelt slung low on his hips, the twin Colts gleaming in the sunlight, their butts rubbed smooth by long use. His hands were like those of a woman's. White and slim fingers, the fingertips always rubbing themselves together as if he held something invisible between his fingers. His face was thin, tight-skinned, with high cheekbones and a thin, cruel slash of a mouth. But it was his eyes that arrested the attention of every man who looked at him. Cold and empty, black-pupilled, devoid of any expression, like those of a rattler poised to strike without warning.

'You'll be Kid Moran,' said Sabine quietly. 'I'm Jed Sabine. Glad you got my message and were able to come.'

The black eyes turned on him. In spite of himself, it was difficult for Sabine to suppress a shiver. It was like looking down into an abyss that had no bottom. Moran inclined his head momentarily in a quick nod.

'You'll be dry after that stage journey,' Sabine said. He waved a hand towards the saloon. 'Let's go there and talk over a drink.'

'Who's this *hombre*?' Moran's voice was flat as he jerked a thumb towards Forrest.

'He's my foreman. He knows about this deal.'

Morans' lips twitched into a faint grin. 'He'd better be the only one who knows. This is a business deal between you and me and the *hombre* you want killed.'

'Sure, sure,' Sabine nodded quickly. 'That's the way it's goin' to be.'

They made their way into the saloon, chose the table furthest from the door. The bartender brought over the whiskey bottle and three glasses, then hurried back to his place behind the counter, picking up the empty glasses there and cleaning them on his apron with fingers that shook a little. Whoever that gunman was that Sabine had brought into town, he meant trouble. That man was a killer if he had ever seen one.

Sabine tossed off the glass of liquor, looked across at Moran. 'I own the biggest spread in these parts,' he said quickly, his face flushed a little. 'Don't matter none how I got it. Only thing that matters now is that this saddlebum has come ridin' in, hornin' in on my plans. He's already shot down my right-hand gun and I want him out of the way, permanently.'

Moran poured a second drink. 'Who is he?' he asked thinly.

'Calls himself Tremaine, Dave Tremaine.' Sabine slid a quick glance towards the bar, then glanced back again. 'That could be his real name, maybe not. I wouldn't know.'

'But you want him killed.' The other seemed to be talking to himself. Then he shrugged. 'I'll do it in my own way and the price is a thousand dollars, payable in advance.'

'A thousand dollars!' Sabine stared at him. 'We agreed on five hundred, and to be paid when the job is finished.' Moran laid his cold glance on Sabine. He said in a sibilant hiss. 'You forgot to mention this *hombre*'s name then. Now you've told me who it is the price has gone up.'

'What's the matter? You suddenly scared of Tremaine?' Forrest spoke out of the side of his mouth.

Moran scarcely seemed to move in his chair, but a split second later, the foresight of one of the Colts was touching the bunch of loose flesh just beneath the foreman's throat. 'I'm scared of nobody,' he said hoarsely. There was a crazed, mad look on his features. 'But some men come higher than others. I've heard of Tremaine even if you ain't. He cleaned up several of the frontier towns south and east of here. He's no two-bit saddlebum if that's what you think of him.' His gaze jerked back to Sabine. 'The price is a thousand dollars. Take it or leave it.'

'All right, all right,' muttered the other placatingly. 'Now simmer down. Forrest didn't mean anythin'.'

Smoothly, Moran slid the weapon back into its holster. He picked up his glass and downed the whiskey quickly. Then he got to his feet, stood staring at Sabine. 'I'll put up at the hotel along the street,' he said. 'Bring the money this afternoon without fail.'

'It'll be there,' Sabine said. He sat quite still at the table and watched the gunman walk out of the saloon, the batwing doors swinging slowly shut behind him. Then he poured himself a third drink, gulped it down.

Hell, but this gunslick was poison. Still, for the first time since Dave Tremaine had showed up in Fenton, he felt confident that everything was going to turn out in his favour after all.

The evening was just passing into night and there was just enough light glimmering in the sky to see the loose bunch of riders as they rode into town from the north-east. Once they hit the end of the road leading through Fenton, they brought their horses down to a quiet walk, but to Dave, watching from the boardwalk outside Doc Keller's, there was something about the wandering gait of the horses that told him these men had ridden far.

As they came closer, he recognized the man in the lead, stepped out of the shadows and hailed him. Lex Corrie urged his mount over towards him, stepped down from the saddle.

'Hoped I'd find you here, Dave,' he said wearily. 'Anythin' happened?'

'Luke stopped a slug in the shoulder. He's in here. Apart from that, things have been mighty quiet around town.' The rest of the men got down, hitched their horses to the nearby rail. 'These are some of the men I told you about,' Corrie said. 'They've agreed to help in stoppin' Sabine.'

Dave let his gaze wander over the group of men clustered in front of the building. There were about a dozen of them. Not enough to meet Sabine and his crew in a straight fight. But then Dave had never expected to defeat the rancher that way. They had to play this with cunning.

'Howdy, boys,' he said, raising a hand in greeting. 'Better step over and get a bite to eat and somethin' to drink at the saloon. But step around easy in town. Sabine rode in this mornin' and he may have some of his crew here.'

He waited until the men had drifted away, then followed Lex into the doctor's surgery.

Dave waited until the older man had had a few words with his son, helped himself to the hot coffee that Roxanna had on the stove. He put in plenty of sugar and milk, drank it hot. It burned his throat but made him feel better. Lex Corrie came over, sat down at the table. He motioned Dave into the chair opposite him, then bent forward and said in a low voice: 'There's word goin' around that Sabine has sent an ultimatum to the mayor here. If they don't shut the town and stop me and the other ranchers movin' our beef through to the railhead, he's sendin' in some of his boys to see they toe the line.'

'So that's to be his next move,' Dave said softly. 'He means to break you all.'

'Knowing Fallon and the rest of the Council here, they won't do a thing to stand up to him. They're scared spitless.'

'And you'll get no help from Sheriff Salmon,' Dave said bitterly.

'I'm goin' along to see Fallon and the others now. I want you to come along with me.' Lex gave a grim smile. 'It might be just possible that we can persuade him in which direction his duty lies.'

'How?'

'If we can make them see that we mean business, that we'll send these coyotes runnin' when they do show up, we might just swing the town behind us against Sabine.' Lex gulped his coffee, grimacing as it scalded his throat on the way down. 'It's the only chance we've got.'

Dave did not feel so confident that things would work out in the way that Lex Corrie hoped; but one thing was certain. If the trail through town to the railhead was blocked for the other ranchers, they might just as well pack up and ride on out, leaving all of the land to Sabine. It was close on a hundred miles to the next railhead and by the time a herd had been pushed all that distance across the Badlands, they would fetch almost nothing at all on the market.

The Fenton Town Council comprised four men. Fallon, the mayor, was a short, bald man with a grey goatee beard, dressed imposingly in a black frock coat and pin-stripe trousers. The other three were Ford Cassidy, one of the bankers, Clem Duprez and Mord Felton.

'I reckon you all know why I'm here,' Lex said harshly. 'To speak up for all of the small ranchers. Sabine is tryin' to close the town to our cattle so we can't get 'em to the railhead and ship 'em out east. You know we've got as much right as he has to bring our beef in.'

'I'm sure we all sympathize with your problem, Mr. Corrie,' said Fallon smoothly. 'But you have to see our predicament too. Either we do as Sabine says, or his men ride in and brace the town. We have to consider the well-being of the citizens of Fenton.'

The way he spoke, Dave reckoned that he had already made up his mind what he, and presumably the Council, intended to do.

'And if we decide to drive our cattle through?' Corrie said. 'Wouldn't take much to stampede 'em into the main street.'

'Are you tryin' to threaten us, Corrie?' muttered Cassidy. 'You know you don't stand a chance against Sabine or you'd have done somethin' about it a long time ago.'

Corrie grinned. 'Guess you ain't heard yet, Cassidy. We've got ourselves somebody who can use a gun as well as any of Sabine's men. Cantry's dead. Sabine's night-hand gun.'

'And you figure that you can stop his men when they come into town tomorrow? He'll send thirty or forty men and you can't stop 'em all – even with this man standin' with you.' He glanced at Dave as he spoke, letting his gaze wander over the other's gunbelt, noticing the smooth butt of the Colt in the holster.

'I've cleaned up towns as rotten as this,' Dave said quietly. There was a note of authority in his voice now. 'Ain't no need to meet Sabine's men head on. Like you say, that'd be foolish. But there are other ways. All we ask is that you give us the chance to show that Sabine can be stopped. You men aren't fools. You know what it's goin' to be like in Fenton when Sabine runs the town.'

'He already runs it,' Corrie broke in, his tone angry. 'Salmon is in cahoots with him. Sabine gives the orders and the Sheriff sees to it that they're carried out.'

'Because we have no other choice,' broke in Fallon heatedly. 'I notice you ranchers haven't done anythin' in the past whenever he's moved in and taken you over. We can't risk havin' the town burned down around our ears. And that's what will happen tomorrow if we don't agree to what Sabine asks.'

'Just keep everybody off the streets tomorrow when they come,' Dave said persuasively. 'And don't mention this little meeting to Salmon. If we send those coyotes runnin' back with their tails between their legs, will you stand with us and fight Sabine? Make this a town where decent men and women can live in peace instead of havin' to knuckle under to a killer like Jed Sabine?'

He saw the look of indecision that flashed over the faces of the four men. Quickly, he pressed home his advantage, knew they were wavering. 'If you let Sabine go on as he is doin', he won't rest until he's squeezed every last drop of wealth from this town. He'll be the law here. Believe me, I've seen towns taken over by gunmen like this. Sooner or later, there's a blood battle in which plenty of innocent men and women get hurt. All because the citizens didn't stand up to these men in the first place.'

'And you honestly think that you and the men you have with you can stop these killers?'

'We can try,' Corrie said. 'They won't be figurin' on any trouble. Could be they'll be so confident we can take 'em by surprise.'

Fallon licked his lips. He was no fool, Dave decided; but he was still a frightened man, and maybe with good reason. So far, in this play, no one, had tried to stand up to Sabine, except perhaps Roxanna, and when all of her hired hands had run out on her, it hadn't been possible for her to go on fighting alone.

'All right,' he said finally, swallowing hard. 'I'm prepared to give you your chance. God knows why, though. It ain't even a chance.'

'Don't be a fool,' snapped Duprez. 'Nothin's goin to stop these men bracin' this town if we don't meet that ultimatum. Best thing for everybody concerned is for you men' – he stared hotly at Dave and Corrie – 'to light a shuck out of town right away. It'll be the coroner's job to handle you by tomorrow mornin' if you stay here, and then we'll be next!'

SEVEN

GUNSMOKE SHOWDOWN

The look-out came running back along the street, his spurred heels kicking up the white dust, a little after ten o'clock the next morning. Dave and Lex Corrie were in the small diner and Dave looked up sharply as he heard the sound of hurried footsteps on the boardwalk outside. The man pushed open the door, came in breathing heavily.

'They're headin' this way, Mr. Tremaine,' he said harshly.

'How many are there?' Dave snapped, getting to his feet.

'About fifteen I'd guess. They're a mile or so away, just headin' for the bridge.'

'Comin' up fast?'

The other shook his head. 'Nope. They seem to be takin' their time.'

That made sense, Dave thought as he buckled on the gunbelt. They would never dream that anyone would have the nerve to stand against them when they rode into town. It was just a matter of coming in as Sabine had

121

ordered, getting the mayor and Town Council to agree publicly to stop anyone else from driving their cattle through to the railhead, then heading for the saloon and washing the trail dust out of their throats before heading back to Sabine with the news.

'All right.' Dave turned to Corrie. 'You know what to do. Get your men in position.'

'You're sure you'll be all right? Don't forget that gunman Sabine hired to kill you might be somewhere in town.'

'I'll remember.' Dave nodded tersely. 'Now get up there and watch for my signal.'

'What about openin' fire?' asked Lex.

'Use your own judgement on that,' Dave told him. 'If it looks like they mean to use their guns, then shoot. But I don't want anybody cuttin' loose just for the sheer hell of it.'

Lex went out. From the doorway, Dave watched him move swiftly across the dusty street, then hitched the gunbelt higher about his waist, moved across to the counter. The stout man in the dirty apron eyed him curiously for a moment, then said: 'You goin' ahead with this crazy idea of yours, mister?'

'You know of any better way of stoppin' Sabine?'

'I know of a lot more ways of stayin' alive,' grunted the other. 'You're one of these tough boys from the east, aren't you? You know everything. You're the *hombre* who can't be told.' He shrugged. 'I've seen a score of men like you ride into Fenton and they all ended up on the mortuary slab. We buried 'em up yonder in the cemetery.'

Dave ignored the other's outburst. He pointed to the wall just behind the counter. 'I'd like to borrow that scattergun of yours,' he said brusquely. 'A Colt is all right, but I've known plenty of men stand up against one. It's quick and damned clean and they figure there's always the chance you'll miss. But a shotgun is a different matter. Nobody is fool enough to think he can get away from that.'

Reluctantly, the other reached out and handed the gun over the counter. Dave checked that it was loaded, hefted it into his left hand and slipped out of the door, moving into the shadowed alley that ran alongside the building. There was a hot breeze sighing along the alley, the air filled with the sharp-smelling dust that the wind had picked up. The air seemed to have been drawn over a furnace before it reached him.

Dave switched his mind from the discomfort as he picked out the sound of hoofbeats at the far end of the main street. They rode in a bunch, moving close together with Forrest, Sabine's foreman at their head. As the lookout had said, they seemed to be in no hurry, moved at a slow trot. Through narrowed eyes, Dave watched them as they approached. They were a tough-looking bunch. He noticed a couple of young hellions, wearing flashy clothes, gaily-coloured kerchiefs around their throats, sitting easily in the saddle, eyes watchful and alert, switching from side to side as they rode. Forrest rode casually, expecting no trouble, but clearly a little worried by the empty street that stretched in front of them as far as the eye could see, with only an occasional mangy dog loping from one side to the other, vanishing into one of the dark alleys that opened off the main street.

The men riding behind Forrest were of all shapes and sizes, old, leather-featured men, and youngsters who considered themselves to be real gunmen. But they all had one thing in common. Each man had been specially chosen by Sabine as a cold-blooded killer who obeyed orders without question.

Forrest turned to the man riding alongside him, said something in a low undertone. The other uttered a harsh, cruel laugh, pulled a sixgun from its holster and sent a couple of shots through the window of the diner. Glass tinkled on to the boardwalk. The man laughed again and Dave reckoned it was time he horned in.

He stepped out of the alley into broad daylight. At first

no one saw him. Then the man with the gun in his hand froze suddenly in the saddle. Dave grinned.

'That's right, mister,' he said quietly. 'Just hold it there and there won't be any trouble. Now drop that iron.'

The other hesitated, glanced sideways at Forrest. The foreman's face was twisted with indecision. His deep-set eyes glittered in the sunlight. His eyes were riveted on the scattergun in Dave's hands. Then he said harshly: 'All right, drop it.'

The gun clattered into the dust. Forrest thrust his head forward, staring now directly at Dave. His features were set in tight lines. 'You figurin' on pushin' your nose into our business, Tremaine?'

'The townsfolk have had enough of your kind and your boss,' Dave said. 'We don't want you here.'

'Yeah,' sneered the foreman. 'I don't see anybody backin' up your play, Tremaine. Seems to me that you're overstretchin' your hand a little. You can't take all of us with that shotgun. So what do you intend to do now?'

'I'll give you a minute to turn around and ride on out of here, back to your boss. Tell him the citizens of Fenton don't want any of his brand of justice.'

Forrest was startled at that. It was visible in his face. Then he pulled himself together. 'Why you saddlebum,' he roared. 'We ain't ridin' anywhere. All I've got to do is give the word and every man here will draw on you.'

'Then go ahead and do it,' Dave said evenly.

Forrest stared, lips tight. He clearly didn't know what to say to that. Dave saw that he was worried now; alert for danger, guessing that Dave wouldn't pull a stunt like this unless he had something else up his sleeve. He sat the saddle tensely, like a coiled spring, like a rattler waiting to strike.

'You're talkin' mighty big,' said the young hellion just behind the foreman.

'Sure,' Dave nodded. He jerked his head slightly. 'If you're figurin' on doin' anythin', take a look up at the windows along the street first.'

As one man, their heads lifted, stared up at the upstairs windows of the buildings along either side of the street. When they saw the rifles and Colts levelled on them from either side, they gave up any ideas they may have had of making a fight of it.

'Now you know the score,' Dave said. 'All of you shuck your guns. Let 'em drop and then ride out of here. Next time you come back there won't be any warnin', we'll shoot you down like the curs you are.'

'Next time we come, we'll take this damned town apart, piece by piece and burn it,' Forrest said viciously.

'Get rid of those guns,' Dave warned. 'And hurry! I'm gettin' nervous.'

Sullen-faced, the men dropped their weapons into the dust among their horses' hooves. Dave almost laughed at their faces. They had ridden into town a few minutes before, thinking they had only to browbeat the mayor and the rest of the Council. Instead, they had run into a trap from which they were being forced to crawl. It was an experience they had seldom had before; one they did not like in the least.

Wheeling his mount with an angry jerk on the reins, Forrest turned in the saddle, spat into the dust. 'You've just signed your death warrant, Tremaine. This is the end of the line for you. And it's comin' sooner than you think. A hell of a lot sooner.'

'*Git!*' Dave jerked the scattergun meaningly.

Hands savagely tugging on the bit, Forrest sent his mount rocketing along the street, the rest of his boys following him. The dust settled slowly. Lex and the others came out into the street. Pushing his hat back on to his head, Lex said exultantly: 'You did it, boy! You sent those skunks high-tailin' it out of town like the devil was on their heels.'

'They'll be back,' Dave said soberly. 'They ain't licked just because of this one showdown.'

Fallon, too, was more cautious as he stepped into the sunshine outside the office, a fat cigar clamped between his thick lips. His eyes kept shifting to the end of the street as if he expected Sabine's bunch to come riding back at any moment.

'So you finally scared 'em off,' he acknowledged reluctantly. 'Now what?'

Dave handed the shotgun back to the fat man who had come out of the diner and was examining the smashed window. 'This is the first part of the play,' he said grimly. 'Those *hombres* will ride on back to Sabine and tell him what happened here. Then he's got to make his move. My guess is he'll wait awhile. This is somethin' he never expected. One thing, though, I'd throw Salmon out of office. He's Sabine's man and as long as he's sheriff, you can't trust the law in this town to do what you want it to.'

Even as he spoke, Salmon came striding along the boardwalk, the star on his shirt glinting in the sunlight, his shadow dark and black on the dust as he stepped down into the street. There was a Winchester in his hand. He paused a few feet away, said curtly: 'I'll take over here, Fallon. I warned this *hombre* about startin' trouble in Fenton.' Turning to Dave, he snapped: 'Now walk ahead of me to the jailhouse, Tremaine. I figure we can find some charge against you that'll stick.'

'You're way behind the times, Salmon,' said Corrie harshly. 'This town has decided it's had enough of Sabine and anybody who works for him. We reckon, too, it's about time we got ourselves a proper Sheriff instead of a crooked four-flusher who does only what Jed Sabine tells him.'

For the first time a hint of fear showed on Salmon's beefy face. He let his gaze wander from the faces of the men who had formed a ring around him, to Fallon, 'Now see here, Fallon,' he blustered. 'I'm the law here and if you try to go along with these men, you're makin' the biggest mistake of your life. Sabine won't stand for that, He'll take this town apart when he hears about this and you know it.'

Dave saw Fallon hesitate, knew the other was still unsure of himself. It needed very little to weaken the mayor. The shadow of Jed Sabine lay too thickly over this town for him to be able to stand up to Salmon for long. Deliberately, he unbuckled his gunbelt, draped it over the top of the nearby rail. 'You've been talkin' mighty big around town about what you intend to do to me, Salmon,' he gritted. 'Now put that gun down, shuck your gunbelt, and we'll see just what you can do.'

Salmon licked his lips uneasily. For a moment the thought of using the rifle on Dave was uppermost in his mind, but the sight of the grim-faced men nearby made him realize that this was the last thing he would ever do. Sullenly, he tossed the rifle on to the boardwalk, let his gunbelt fall into the dust. He was a big man, rough and strong. Fallon hurriedly moved back as Dave went forward.

'All right, lawman.' There was derision in Dave's voice. 'Let's see how you fare against a man without a gun to back you up.'

Snarling viciously, Salmon hurled himself forward, flying at Dave in a sudden jump, head lowered. He was very fast, much faster than Dave had thought. The bullet-like head hammered hard into Dave's side, knocking him on to his back. Rearing up, Salmon hammered a second blow with his fist at Dave's face, the knuckles grazing the skin as he twisted his head sharply. Then the taloned fingers were at his throat, squeezing with all the strength in the wiry hands.

Dave couldn't get up. Salmon's face stared down at him with the sun behind him, his eyes crazy with hate, features flushed with a look of triumph. Desperately, Dave struggled to drag air down into his tortured, heaving lungs. Lights flashed in front of his eyes and he could feel them beginning to bulge from their sockets as the terrible pressure increased. He knew that he would have to break the other's fanatical hold or die.

It took all he had, but he managed to get his arms

inside the other's. With a savage outward thrust, he broke the other's hold on his throat, reared up on to his side, throwing Salmon off.

With a harsh smell of the dust in his nostrils and the pain in his chest, he didn't want to get up. Salmon had fallen on to his side, winded by the impact, but not badly hurt. Slowly, Dave pulled himself to his feet, saw through dazed eyes that Salmon was already on his, looming over him, seemingly a mile high as he stood against the vicious glare of the sun. He lifted one foot, the boot with its great iron spur hovering over Dave's shoulders. Then the Sheriff's foot came down with all of his weight behind it, seeking to smash his ribs and cripple him for good and all. Rolling sideways in the dust, he snaked a grip on the man's ankle as the boot came down, twisted with all of the strength left in him. Salmon uttered a high-pitched wailing cry as he fell off balance, arms flailing madly as he went down. A cloud of white dust lifted from the street and stung the back of Dave's nostrils as he pushed himself upright. Sucking air into his lungs, he waited for the other to get up. Swaying a little, eyes blinking in the sunglare, Salmon came forward again, but this time he had grown more wary. Dirt and blood were smudged across his face and his lips were swollen, mouth twisted into a grimace of pure hate. He had taken a beating, but there was still plenty of strength left in his body.

He was wicked and vicious with temper, too, no longer cared what happened to him so long as he inflicted damage on his opponent. Dave stopped his forward rush with a couple of hard blows to the head, but they seemed to do little damage; the other merely shook his head as if to throw off their effect. His hat had fallen from his head, his hair hanging down over his eyes. The next time he came in, he feinted with his left, then kicked at Dave, his toe catching him just above the right knee, laming him for the time being. Seizing his chance, Salmon threw himself forward like a wildcat, striking with his fists, feet, nails, butting with his head. All the time he was muttering whiningly in his throat, teeth showing in his face.

Dave waited, his brain clear now. As the other sprang at him, he met him with a right-hand punch, flush on the face. Cartilage squashed under his knuckles and blood spurted from the Sheriff's nose. Another hard blow to the point of the chin as the man staggered, sent him whirling around, to fall against the wooden rails, legs folding under him. He lay still, his eyes open, chest rising and falling as the breath rasped in and out of his lungs. The star had been torn from his shirt during the fight and lay in the dust a few feet away.

After a while, when the other made no attempt to move, Dave went over to him, slapping the dust off his shirt. He was less than three feet away when Salmon's right hand moved, swiftly, reaching out for the Colt in the holster where it had been dropped at the beginning of the fist-fight. Dave moved instinctively. His booted heel came down on the other's wrist. There was the crackling snap of bones being broken. Salmon let out a blubbering scream, clutched at his smashed wrist, holding it to him.

'Get your bronc and ride out of town,' Dave said dispassionately. Bending, he hitched his own gunbelt around his cuddle.

Turning on his heel, he made to walk away, paused as Fallon called to him. There was the silver badge in his hand which he had picked up from the dust where it had fallen.

'Mr Tremaine.' There was a new note of authority in his voice. 'I ain't sure how many of the townsfolk I'm speakin' on behalf of right now, but I want you to take this. Make the authority of it stand until we get a chance to elect ourselves a new Sheriff. After what's happened, all hell can break loose in Fenton in the next few days, unless we've got a star here to hold things in line and a man who can back it up with action.'

Dave hesitated. 'You're sure you know what you're doin'offerin' this badge to me? There's to be no backin' out on the deal if I take this, no stoppin' until Sabine and his men have been smashed.'

'The town's committed now, Tremaine,' muttered the other. He pinned the star on Dave's shirt.

'I hope you've figured one thing, Fallon,' Dave said grimly. 'With me wearin' this star there are a few in town who won't admit the authority of it.'

'Then you'll have to make 'em admit it,' Fallon said. His eyes turned on Salmon for a moment as the other picked himself up and shambled across the street. 'It's taken a lot to have our eyes opened. You've got a free hand now.'

Darkness was settling in when Dave Tremaine made his circuit of the town. He deliberately walked along the middle of the street and with every step he took the brooding stillness that was Fenton, settled deeper and deeper around him. There was that peculiar little itch just in the middle of his shoulders that he had experienced on several occasions in the past when he had carried out a similar chore to this in some other hell-town along the frontier. With an effort, he reminded himself that a shoulder was no good in stopping a .45 slug and forced himself to relax, his eyes and ears attentive, picking up every little movement and sound.

Half an hour earlier, after Salmon had ridden out of town, he had checked at the livery stables asking about any strangers who may have ridden into town that day, but there had been none. The groom there had been emphatic about that. A further check at the stage depot had elicited that there had been five passengers come in on the stage that morning and that Jed Sabine and his foreman had been there to meet someone who had got off. They had gone off with the stranger into the saloon and twenty minutes later the man had booked in at the hotel along the street. As far as the clerk knew, nobody had seen the stranger since then.

Dave pondered on that piece of information as he strode slowly along the dusty river of the main street, then cut along one of the alleys into a wilderness in which smashed boxes and bottles were the only vegetation. It sure sounded as if the killer that Sabine had hired was already in town, deliberately keeping himself out of sight for the time being, probably watching him from his room at the hotel, making his own plans. Dave experienced a tight feeling at the thought, then thrust it away. He would simply have to be ready for when Kid Moran made his play.

Entering the main street at the far end of the town, he glanced quickly as a buckboard, flanked by three men on horseback swung into sight around the corner near the livery stables. The turning wheels threw up little clouds of dust that were whipped away by the evening breeze. Narrowing his eyes, Dave stepped towards it.

The driver, a tall, black-bearded man hauled up on the reins. The woman beside him stared straight ahead, her face set in lines of grief. Then Dave glanced down into the back of the buckboard, saw the body that lay under the heavy sheet.

Quietly, he said: 'What happened?'

The tall man turned his head. For a moment he said nothing, then his eyes lit on the star on Dave's shirt, widened a little. 'Where's Ben Salmon,' he asked in a toneless voice.

'He's no longer around,' Dave told him. 'There've been a few changes in town today. The folk decided they'd had enough of Sabine runnin' the place. They made me temporary Sheriff.'

'Then I reckon you're the man we want to see.' His tone was soft, but there was steel underneath it. 'A bunch of Sabine's killers jumped us at the ranch this afternoon. They herded us outside, then fired the place, drove off the cattle. Tom, our son, tried to stop 'em, so they shot him. He never had a chance, never even had a gun, but I figure that don't mean anythin' to killers like them.'

Dave nodded. 'That all of it?'

'Ain't no more to tell. Maybe we should've sold out when Sabine made his last offer. Now we got nothin'.'

The woman's mouth twisted still further but she still stared straight ahead of her into the darkness, as if she were carved out of stone. In a faint whisper she said: 'Murderers! They'd kill anyone, even an unarmed, defenceless boy. Why isn't there any law in this country?'

'There is now,' Dave said gravely. He made to say something more, but the black-bearded man cut him off.

'You reckon you can stand against Sabine and his crew?' There was a note of astonished incredulity in his voice.

'We're goin' to do our best.'

The other pondered that for a moment, brows pulled together. Then he jerked a hand towards the men sitting quietly in the saddle by the buckboard. 'Seth and the boys will help. I never figured I'd live to see the day when somebody said they was goin' to stand up to Sabine. I'll do what's right by Tom, get Ethel a place to stay and then join you. Guess you need every gun you can get.'

Dave raised his right hand in acknowledgment, then stood on one side as the small group rode past. It was beginning to look as if Sabine was already makng his play. Maybe he figured that if he attacked and took over as many of these small ranches and homesteads as he could, it would strengthen his hand when it came to the showdown with Fenton. He must have known that there was just a chance of the smaller men throwing in their lot with the citizens of the town once they heard of the latest developments there and he meant to chase them clear of the territory before they could do this.

But in doing this it was more than likely that he had been forced to split his forces. He would not commit all of his men to the task of chasing out the little men around Fenton. The thought grew stronger in Dave's mind. Turning, he made his way quickly along the street, saw the buckboard standing outside the mortuary. There was no sign of the woman.

Even as Dave came up to the place, the black-bearded man came out, glanced up and saw him. He paused with his hand on the reins.

'The boys are over in the saloon, Sheriff,' he said, nodding across the street. 'You wantin' to see them?'

'Could be,' Dave said. 'After that bunch hit your ranch, you got any idea where they were headed next?'

'They said somethin' about Sam Egger's place. That's over on the far side of the valley, to the south.'

'Could be it'll take 'em a little while to get there.'

'Sure,' nodded the other. 'You got somethin' on your mind, Sheriff?'

'If we can take that bunch, we can whittle down Sabine's strength. How many of those sidewinders do you reckon hit your place?'

'About a dozen.'

'You willin' to ride out with us in twenty minutes?'

'Sure,' said the other without hesitation. 'I'll get Seth and the boys together.' He hurried over to the saloon. Dave moved towards the Sheriff's office to get Lex Corrie and the rest of the men.

They rode south-east from Fenton, Dave Tremaine leading the way with Lex beside him. He felt bone tired, for it had been a long, tiring day, but he urged his mount on as fast as it would go without any trouble, without even pausing to think about the aches and bruises in his body, because this was not something new as far as he was concerned. He could not even begin to count the number of times in the past when he had ridden a hard, long ride through the night after having had no sleep for two or three days. It was part of his job, something he looked upon as a necessary part of his work.

They rode through the darkness without rest, fording
the narrow, swift-running streams that cut through the
wastelands in this direction. Shortly before two o'clock
in the morning they bumped into four men spurring
their mounts towards them. Dave slid his Colt from its
holster, held up a hand to halt the posse, waited until
the men were almost level with them, then called on
them to halt.

The others reined up instantly, hands moving down
towards their guns, then pausing as they saw that Dave had
the drop on them. Lex moved closer to the others, then
called back.

'It's Sam Egger and three of his men, Dave.'

Holstering the gun, Dave edged his mount forward.
He said tightly: 'You seen anythin' of Sabine's men,
Egger?'

'You're damned right we have,' snarled the other.
'They drove off my herd less than an hour ago. Right now
they're firing the ranch. Ain't nothin' we can do about it.
Too many of 'em for us to handle. We was ridin' back to
Fenton for help. Not that we'll get any there.'

'The help's here,' Dave said sharply. 'We heard that
Sabine's men might be ridin' out to your place. Seems
we're too late to stop 'em destroying the ranch, but we
might by able to hit 'em before they finish the job.'

'Now you're talkin,' said Egger harshly. He motioned to
his men to swing in behind the others.

Mounting a low rise, they came upon the valley where
Egger's ranch was situated. It was impossible to miss it
even in the darkness. Two of the outbuildings were already
burning and by the light of the leaping flames, it was possible to make out the horses tethered in the courtyard, well
back from the house, and the dark shapes of the men
moving around.

'We'll dismount here and move in on 'em from all
sides,' Dave said. 'I want to get close enough to spook
those horses before we start shootin'. Lex, spread the

men out and cover me, but no shootin' until you see me signal.'

'You're a crazy fool if you reckon you can get down there without bein' seen,' said Corrie thinly. 'You'll get yourself killed sure as little apples.'

'Just you see to it that the men are in position and ready to open fire,' Dave said stubbornly. 'I'll take care of myself.'

The ground ahead of him was bare, with only a few scratches of vegetation and one or two stunted bushes and cacti. He took it slow, keeping his head and shoulders down, crawling most of the way on his hands and knees. The crackling of the flames as they took a firm hold on the barn and bunkhouse, and the occasional shrill yells of the men, drowned out any noise he might be making. But the flooding lurid glow spread out by the fires lit up the scene almost as bright as day. It needed only one of the men to turn and see him and all hell would be let loose.

There was no chance at all of finishing these men off slick and easy. Even if taken by surprise, they would fight furiously. Inch by inch, he slithered forward on his belly, all of the aches and bruises crowding in on him now, making themselves felt. By now, he was about ten yards from the line of horses, knew he could get no further without exposing himself. The ground ahead was completely bare, with no cover at all. Gathering his legs beneath him, he threw himself forward, raced towards the horses. Reaching them, he dropped on to his knees in the dirt; but he had been seen. One of the men, glancing into the darkness behind him had caught the sudden movement. He yelled a fierce warning to the others, snapped off a couple of shots, the slugs whining with a shrill shriek off the hard, sun-baked ground.

Instinct urged Dave to fire back. But he fought it down. Reaching up with his right hand, he loosened the knot that held the long rope through the bridles of the horses.

There was the sound of feet running towards him. The rope came free. Swiftly he fired a shot into the air. The nearest horse reared up, pawing at the air in its fright. The next moment the long line of them had jerked their heads away from the rail and were stampeding off into the flame-stained darkness.

As lead smacked and whizzed into the ground around him, Dave wriggled back, snaking over the flat, smooth ground. Silhouetted against the glare, he saw three men converging on him. The courtyard thundered with gunfire, the hammering pulse of the weapons making a vast turmoil of noise that crashed against his eardrums, making the air shudder about him. Light fingers seemed to pluck at his clothing as he squirmed back towards the cover of the bushes. Lead cracked terrifyingly against the wooden upright. A splinter of oak cut him across the cheek, drawing blood. He could feel it trickling slowly down the side of his face.

With his Colt levelled he squeezed off several shots at the running men. One threw up his arms high over his head as though clutching at something invisible there to hold on to, then slumped drunkenly. Another was hit in the belly, the leaden impact forcing him to his knees as he skidded along the dusty ground. The third man seemed to leap high into the air as he screamed once, his voice high-pitched with mortal agony.

Scarcely had Dave got away from the scene than the rifles and Colts of the posse opened up, adding their din to the hideous racket. One or two of them were a mite close to where he lay, but he could see Sabine's men scattering as the storm of lead poured into them. The night was alive with the crash of guns and the screams of dying and wounded men. The men who had run to take cover inside the ranch, were soon forced out into the open again as the fire which they had started caught at the walls and roof.

Dave grinned viciously to himself. These men had signed their own death warrants by their very act of destroying the ranch and outbuildings. A man came staggering blindly out of the front door of the ranch, his body high-lighted by the flames at his back as they roared and flicked along the wooden uprights. He was firing as he stumbled down into the courtyard, his thin mouth drawn back into a wicked grin. Then a slug hit him, spun him round, pitching him on to his back, his legs drumming on the hard earth as a man almost always does when he had been gutshot. For several seconds he squirmed on the ground, clutching at his belly, then collapsed in a heap, unmoving. Another man, yelling at the top of his voice came out of the house. For a moment, he stood on the smouldering porch, shooting blindly into the darkness. Then he, too, was hit. Turning, he walked drunkenly along the porch, into the wall at the far end, tipped forward on to his toes as he tried to put out his hands to lean against it and steady himself, then coughed, a stream of blood pulsing from his lips as he slid down out of sight.

Getting to his feet, Dave ran back to where Corrie was crouched between a couple of large boulders, flung himself down beside the other. The muscles of his stomach were drawn tight and there was sweat on his body in spite of the coldness of the night.

Reloading his Colt, he lay still and peered into the smoke and flame that now shrouded the ranch-house. There seemed to be only a couple of guns still firing down there, but his ears were still ringing from the terrible beat of the gunfire and it was difficult for him to make out sounds properly. Cornie loosed off several shots as another figure broke cover, driven out into the courtyard by the smoke and flames. But he missed and the man ran on, threw himself down behind the long horse trough.

Ten minutes later it was all over. No further sound came from the blazing buildings. The fire had taken a firm hold and there was no chance at all, Dave saw, of extinguishing it. Slowly, the men made their way down into the valley,

their eyes alert, watchful for trouble. His gun in his hand,
Dave strode forward, saw only one brief movement at the
edge of his vision, whirled instinctively, cat-like, the gun in
his hand fanning on the other.

The man sat with his back against the trough, his body
twisted. There was a dark, irregular stain on the front of
his shirt and his breathing was harsh and rasping in his
throat. He had a gun in his hand, was trying with a
desperate strength to lift it and bring the barrel to bear
on Dave as he moved forward, steadying his limp hand by
grasping the wrist with his other hand. He was clearly in
agony with the lead burning deep within him, his whole
body convulsed with the effort. Dave saw the tip of the
gun barrel come up, a little at a time, saw the sweat standing out on the other's gleaming face, the look at the back
of the dark eyes. Dave waited almost patiently, then fired
a single shot. The man's body shuddered all over, jerked
back against the trough. The gun dropped from dead
fingers, lay beneath him as he toppled over. Going
forward, Dave turned him over with his boot, but the
man was gone. With a faint sigh, he straightened up,
sucking air into his lungs. He thrust the gun back into its
holster.

Egger came around the side of the burning ranch-
house, his face twisted into a grimace. 'All gone,' he said
dully. Anger beat in his tone. 'But we finished them
coyotes, every last one of 'em is dead.'

'You'll be able to build yourself another ranch,' Dave
said. 'Once we've run Sabine out of our territory. I figure
that most of his cattle belong to the smaller ranchers
around here.'

Corrie came up, looked at the dead man lying by the
horse trough. His lips twisted a little. 'Hell, but this is sure
goin' to hit Sabine bad when he hears of it. He won't be
able to stop and make any plans. He'll have to hit us and
hit us quick. Those men who ride with him are low-down
killers, and they won't ride with a man who loses. They'll
fork their broncs and ride on over the hill lookin' for

another master to serve who'll prove strong enough to back his threats with force.'

'Let's get back to Fenton,' Dave said harshly. He walked away from the silent courtyard and the flames leaping high into the night sky. Just as they were riding over the lip of the valley, the roof of the ranch-house collapsed inward in a shower of sparks and a rumbling roar.

EIGHT

THE PAY-OFF

They pushed their horses hard and rode into Fenton just before daybreak. Reining up in front of the Sheriff's office, they climbed down stiffly from their mounts. Dave looked about him, along the deserted street in either direction. A swamper was on the point of stepping out of the Broken Lance saloon, a birch broom in his hands. He threw a curious glance at the men clustered in front of the jailhouse, then shrugged, started to brush away the dirt from the boardwalk with glow, lazy movements of the broom.

'I guess you could all do with a bite to eat, boys,' Dave said quietly. He nodded towards the saloon. 'Wake somebody up yonder and tell 'em I sent you. Least this town can do is feed us after our night's work.'

The men grinned tiredly, moved across the street. Lex Corrie waited, went into the office with Dave, sat down heavily in the chair in front of the desk and put his feet up.

'You heard anythin' about Kid Moran yet, Dave?' he asked in a quiet tone. 'There's talk that he rode into town on yesterday's stage.'

'So I heard.' Dave nodded, sat down in the high-backed chair opposite the other. He seemed outwardly unconcerned by the threat that the presence of the killer imposed.

'He'll make his move soon. Maybe sooner than you figure once he hears that Sabine has been hit hard. He probably collected his blood money in advance, but knowin' the sort of man he's reputed to be, I'm mighty certain he'll try to earn it.'

'I'm sure he will.' Dave opened a drawer in the desk, brought out a bottle of whiskey and two glasses, set them down in front of him and poured a couple of drinks.

'Be careful, son,' said Corrie warningly as he tossed down the whiskey. 'You may be fast and this night's work may have gone to your head, but just you remember that you can't win all of 'em. There's sure to come a time when lady luck runs out on you just when you need her most. I wouldn't like this to be the time. This Kid Moran is a killer, I've heard of him from all towns clear to the border. He's got a string of killings to his name, all of 'em men who figured they was fast with a gun.'

Dave nodded slowly. The other was genuinely worried. He could see that. It felt a little strange to have someone else worry about him. He finished the whiskey, made to pour himself a second glass, then thought better of it and pushed the bottle away from him.

Footsteps sounded on the creaking wooden boardwalk outside. A moment later there came a knock on the door. One of the men who had ridden with them during the night came in. He said, almost apologetically:

'There's a *hombre* over in the saloon right now, Mr, Tremaine, says he'd be obliged if you'd step into the street sometime. He says he's got somethin' to settle with you.'

Dave raised his brows a little. 'Did this *hombre* give any name?' he asked, his voice level.

'Yeah, Sheriff. He says it's Kid Moran. He says you'll know what he means.'

'Go back and tell him I'll be out in a couple of minutes. We don't want to keep a polecat like that waitin'.'

After the other had gone, Corrie said harshly: 'You want me to come with you, Dave? Ain't no way of tellin' how this critter will go about this. He may even have somebody stashed away in one of the alleys or up at the windows, ready to plug you in the back when he faces up to you.'

Dave shook his head, hitched the gunbelt up a little, tightening it by a single notch. Taking out the Colt, he spun the chamber, checked that it was loaded, then thrust it back into the holster.

'Like you said before, Lex. He's got a certain reputation to keep up. Won't do that any good unless he was to meet me face to face. I figure I know how he operates.'

'OK. But I still think you're mad goin' up against him. He's real poison.'

It was almost as if Dave had not heard him. Brushing past the other, he moved to the door, opened it, then stepped out on to the boardwalk. There was a long streak of grey in the east now, where the dawn was brightening, plenty of light to see by, but not to be too sure of what you saw. Evidently Moran had chosen this time of day to suit himself. There was one other thing that Dave realized the moment he stepped outside.

He had his back to the dawn. He was highlighted against it, whereas Moran would be moving towards him still in shadow. Clearly the other was not so all-fired sure of himself, but had to make everything possible be to his advantage, seeking to gain every bit of edge on him he could.

There was a square of yellow light showing above the batwing doors of the saloon. A few men were in sight now further along the street. Word semed to have got around of what was afoot, for they kept their distance, but they were obviously there to see what the outcome of this gun battle was going to be.

Slowly, Dave stepped down into the dusty street, every nerve tensed and alert. He seemed to be hearing things far more clearly now. The faint creak of a faded sign in the wind fifty yards along the street. The whinney of a horse down in front of the smithy further away still. Then, too, there was the endless thumping of his heart against his ribs.

For several moments, nothing moved. The silence was a heavy thing, hard and tangible, so that it weighed on him like a great, breathing animal crouched at his back. Then the swing doors were pushed open and Kid Moran stepped through. Dave watched him silently through narrowed lids. The other was a dark shape once the doors had shut behind him, with only his head and shoulders visible against the light above them.

Then he stepped down into the street, moved away from the boardwalk, an indistinct shadow against the darkness behind him.

'I hear you've been lookin' for me, Moran,' Dave called. 'Heard that Sabine had to bring in a cheap gunhawk to try to run me out of town because he ain't a big enough man to make a try for it himself.'

There was a pause as the silence built up again, then Moran called softly: 'Go ahead and talk if you want to, Tremaine. I've heard all about you. Maybe it'll interest you to know, before you die, that I got a thousand dollars in my pocket here for this job.'

Dave grinned. 'You ain't earned it yet.'

'No, but that's goin' to be fixed very soon.' He came forward, a step at a time, his hands hovering close above the butts of his guns. He walked with a gunman's slouch, his shoulders thrust forward a little so that he had only a short distance to reach for the weapons. 'How does it feel to be starin' death in the face like this?'

Dave said nothing, waited as the other edged along the street. He had the feeling that for all his brag and loud talk, the other was a trifle unsure of himself. Perhaps he, too, was thinking that somewhere along the trail, in some frontier town such as this, he might come up against a man who was just a shade faster than he was, who might beat him to the draw.

'Just keep walkin', Moran,' Dave said finally, when the other was less than ten yards away. 'Every step you take brings you closer to death. You've taken Sabine's blood money, now let everybody in town see if you can earn it.'

Moran stopped. Scowling a little, he snarled. 'You so impatient to die? I want to see you squirm, to turn and run. I've seen men who talked as big as you do the same.'

'Then it's too bad that you're goin' to be disappointed.'

Moran started talking again in a low voice, as if to himself. Dave ignored him, kept his eyes fixed on the man's face, on his eyes, watching him with an unfocused stare that would take in every movement he made. He knew that this was an old trick, trying to distract his attention from his gunhand.

Moran made his play a moment later, pivoting as if to turn away, then jerking upright, snatching for his guns, jerking them from their holsters and squeezing the triggers in the same movement, his hands a blur of speed. To the men on the boardwalks, watching the gunplay, it seemed that three guns spoke in unison, with the echoes of shots racing down the street in a continuous roar of sound.

When the smoke cleared, Moran was bent almost double, knees folding under him as if no longer able to bear his weight. One of the slugs he had fired had smashed the other window of the diner along the street, the second ploughing into the dust a few feet from where Dave stood, his gun lowered on the other as the killer sagged to his knees, remained upright on them, head lifted, staring in mute astonishment at the man who stood over him, a look of stunned amazement written on his thin, hawk-like features. He struggled to get his guns up again, but the barrels dropped downward as if they were too heavy for his wrists to lift. Lips drawn back in a vicious, bestial snarl, he tried to get some words out, but a red foam gushed from his mouth and he toppled over on to his side, his eyes glazing in the grey dawn light that now began to flood along the street.

Holstering the gun, Dave said to one of the watching men: 'Get him into the morgue and have the coroner see him. I guess we can find a spot for him up there in the cemetery.'

'Sure thing.' Two men came forward, lifted Moran's lifeless body and carried it into one of the nearby buildings.

'Hell,' breathed Corrie, coming up beside Dave. 'I swear I ain't never seen shootin' like that in my life.'

'This is only the beginnin'. News of this is goin' to reach Sabine pretty soon. Then he'll have to act. My guess is that he'll collect all of his men together and ride on the town. We don't have much time to make preparations.'

Heat boiled up in the streets of Fenton, hung in a shimmering, dusty wave over everything. The white-washed walls of the houses on the outskirts threw back the harsh glare so that it dazzled and hurt the eyes. Not that there were many men abroad at high noon in the town. The streets and alleys were empty but for a few mangy curs.

Dave Tremaine stepped out of the Sheriff's office, lit the cigarette between his lips, glanced along the street from beneath hooded lids. Through the shivering heat haze, he could just make out the figure of the man on the roof of the building at the very end of the street. From there, a man could see right out over the river, across the flat land that lay beyond, where the trail wound over the hills in the far distance. If Sabine was coming to brace the town, that was the direction from which it was most likely he would come.

Dragging the smoke down into his lungs, he made his way slowly along the boardwalk. The deep-seated weariness was still in his body and movement made it feel a little better.

Corrie came out of the saloon, crossed the street towards him, spurs lifting little puffs of alkali dust with every step he took. 'No sign of those critters,' said the older man harshly. He wiped his lips with the back of his sleeve.

Dave shook his head sombrely. 'They'll be here soon. Just as soon as they pluck up their courage.'

'And you're sure we'll be ready for 'em? What if the

townfolk don't stand behind us and back our play? I figure it wouldn't be too wise to trust Fallon and those other old goats on the Council to stick to their words.'

'Then we shall just have to fight it out ourselves.' Dave stared off into, the harsh glaring sunlight. There were few shadows in the street now with the sun a fiery disc, almost directly overhead. 'And I sure hope that whoever it was killed Clem Fordyce is with them too.'

'I'm tellin you, boss, we don't stand a chance if we simply ride into Fenton and try to take the place.' Forrest's tone was pitched a little higher than usual. His face was white under the tan. 'That's just what Tremaine is wantin' us to do. He'll be there with the town standin' right behind him, solid all the way along the main street. We lost half of our men at Egger's place last night.'

'You think I don't realize that?' Sabine chewed at the end of his cigar 'But I'm still runnin' this show and you take the orders I give. Tremaine has stood up against me too long now. I'm goin' to grind him into the dirt along with anyone else who stands with him. As for the townfolk of Fenton, you can forget 'em; all of em. They're just a bunch of rabbits. They won't fight. They'll stay shut away in their houses and wait until the shootin' is finished and then come out.'

'I still say you're takin' too much of a chance,' protested the foreman stubbornly.

'I ain't seen that botherin' you none before now.' Sabine whirled on the other, his eyes blazing fiercely. There was something red and frightening in their depths. 'Now get the boys saddled up and be ready to move out in half an hour. As for you, don't forget I know who shot Clem Fordyce in the back. Tremaine will be lookin' for the polecat who did that.'

'How'd you know he still don't think that Luke Corrie did it?'

Sabine grinned viciously. 'From what I hear, Corrie was wounded when Tremaine bumped into him and Shorty on

the north pasture. Seems that it was Shorty who tried to
kill Corrie. Tremaine took him back to Doc Keller's and
he's makin' a good recovery. That looks to me as if
Tremaine has believed his story. So he'll be out lookin' for
some other *hombre*. I figure that by now he knows it wasn't
me, and everythin' is beginnin' to point right at you.'
Sabine's tone hardened abruptly. 'Now get the boys ready.
I don't want to keep Tremaine and Fenton waiting.'

They rode out of the wide courtyard twenty minutes
later, a tight bunch of men, the cloud of dust that lifted
behind them stretching out like a plume of smoke to their
rear as they headed in the direction of Fenton at a swift
gallop. Sabine rode in the lead with Forrest a little
distance behind. As he rode, Jed Sabine turned over in his
mind all of the things that had happened since that
prospector had been shot in the alley. It had been the
spark that had been needed to light the fuse which led to
the powder keg called Fenton. The place had been ready
to blow sky-high for some time now. But he might have
pulled it all off if it hadn't been for Tremaine. He recognized now that it was either the other or himself. This
stretch of territory just wasn't big enough for the two of
them. One had to go; and he was determined that it was
not going to be him. He had spent too much time and
money building up this sweet little empire he had here to
let it slip through his fingers like this. There was no way of
telling, until he got there, how well Tremaine had stirred
up the townfolk.

There was also Kid Moran to be taken into acount. As
far as he knew, the killer was still there, in Fenton, biding
his time before he made his play. If he got rid of Tremaine
before they rode into town, then it would solve all of his
problems in one fell swoop. It did not occur to him that
Tremaine could outdraw Moran. He had got lucky with
Cantry, but the other had been more of a braggart than a
gunman when it came to facing down someone who knew
how to handle a gun. Moran was a very different kettle of
fish, which was why he had agreed to pay him a thousand

dollars in advance. If he got rid of Tremaine without any fuss it would be money well spent.

They cut across the Badlands, heading among the tall, skyreaching buttes, men and horses dwarfed by the gigantic stone columns, etched and fluted into monstrous, fantastic shapes by long geological ages of wind and dust.

Two hours later, the low foothills loomed in the distance, rising out from the flat ground. It was now almost noon. As soon as they reached the high ground it was possible to see, far off beyond the grade which faced them, standing out clear and almost motionless in the distance, shimmering only a little in the heated air, the town of Fenton. They had swung in a wide circle, were now to the north-west of it. In the dry air that lay close to the ground over the desert, the town seemed only a mile or so away, but Sabine knew it was the best part of two hours hard riding away and in spite of the sloping downgrade, the ground was slashed through with deep crevasses and cut-banks which, from the high ground, were visible only as faint hairline streaks on the otherwise featureless surface.

He watched his men closely when they weren't watching him. A few of them were letting their nervousness show through already and that was not a good sign. He was not sure whether he could still hold them together. The loss of the men who had been sent to burn the small ranches during the previous afternoon and night had been a bitter pill for him to swallow, had impressed on him the fact, inescapable now, that he would have to make his move now, before Tremaine had the chance to rouse the townsfolk of Fenton still further against him. If he showed the slightest sign of weakening now, he was finished, and he knew it.

Winding their way in single file through the short shadows of brush and rock formations, they approached the town. Keyed up, and tensed, Sabine tried to look confident in front of the men riding with him. These men were born killers, would follow him and obey his orders only so long as he proved to them that he was the strongest and biggest man in the territory. The minute someone stepped up to challenge that reputation, they would become watchful, wary.

Sabine's move almost took Tremaine by surprise. When the look-out on the roof at the end of the street failed to spot dust in the distance, he began to get worried. He did not think it likely that Sabine would leave it as long as this before he rode in for the inevitable showdown. The other had nothing to gain and everything to lose by delaying. He had the unshakeable feeling there was something wrong, very wrong. There was often a hot quietness lying over the town at this time of day, when every sensible person went indoors for a siesta, waiting until the sun had dropped a little towards the western horizon before coming out. But this was a very different kind of quiet. It was all tight, all keyed up, poised about them, pressing down on all sides, bringing with it that shaky feeling in the pit of the stomach, knotting the muscles, which always came just before a storm broke. All hell was just getting ready to blow its top.

Acting on impulse, he walked along the quiet, empty street in the opposite direction. Out there, to the north of the town, there was nothing but bare rock and desert. Reaching the outskirts of town, he paused, stared off into the sun-scorched distance. Almost at once, he spotted the dust. It was about two miles off, he reckoned, but it was the sort of dust that a bunch of hard-riding men would lift. Jerking the Colt from its holster, he fired a couple of shots into the air, then ran back towards the square in the middle of town.

There was no sign of Mayor Fallon, or of any of the men who had been promised. Dave looked about him at the faces of the men who stood in the dust, rifles in their hands, Colts thrust into leather holsters. His face was set in grim lines as he said tightly:

'There's dust out yonder to the north. Sabine must've figured we might be settin' a trap for him, so he's ridden around in that direction, maybe hopin' to take us by surprise. I'd like for all of you to spread out and line up on either side of the street. Don't show yourselves until I give the signal. A few of you line the roofs like you did before. They might not fall for it a second time, but we've got nothing to lose. Up there a man has plenty of cover if he keeps his wits about him and doesn't show his head too often.'

The dull tattoo of hoofbeats became audible in the distance a few moments later. Dave made sure the rest of the men were in position, then walked quickly to the boardwalk at the corner of the square where he could watch all of the roads and alleys leading into the middle of town, and settled down with his back and shoulders against the hot wood.

The tightly-knit bunch of men boiled up the street in a canter, and then stopped. Something about the stillness must have hit them right there and then, Dave thought tensely. He noticed that Sabine had more than thirty men at his back. All of the odds were in the other's favour. Even without those men who had been killed at Egger's ranch, he still had the power to smash his way through the town and brace it if he played his cards right. Dave reckoned it was up to him to see that the other didn't get the chance to do so. He knew from past experience of situations such as this in other towns that the only way to keep the enemy on the jump was to give him time to relax and swing the battle in his favour. He saw Sabine with them and a little way behind, Forrest, the foreman. Dave eyed the foreman with a fresh interest. Could he be the man who had killed Clem? he wondered tightly. There were several things which pointed to it now that he knew for sure that Luke Corrie had had no part in the other's murder. Kid Moran hadn't been around then and Cantry was not the sort who would lower himself to shoot a man in the back, especially a man who could not handle a gun.

So that left Sabine or Forrest. Sabine could certainly have done it. He would, in the end, have been the man who had given the order. Dave mulled that over in his mind. That being so, he decided, Sabine would certainly have passed on the dirty work to one of his men. Which left only Forrest.

He put the thought out of his mind as Sabine suddenly yelled: 'If you're around any place, Tremaine, better step out here and get this over with before I lose my patience and burn the town.'

Dave stepped out into the open, the Colt in his hand levelled on the big man's chest. 'Freeze right there,' he said. 'Right now you're holding a busted flush and not the aces you figured you had.'

Sabine froze. Two of his men moved their hands instinctively towards their guns, then stopped the downward movement of their hands as the Colt moved slightly to cover them. Sabine glared at the pistol, swallowed, then said thinly: 'You don't have a chance and you know it, Tremaine.' He paused, went on: 'I see they've even pinned on Salmon's star. You supposed to be the law in town now?'

'I guess you could say that,' Dave agreed. 'Just in case you're figurin' on doin' anythin' stupid, you'd better take a look up there.'

The men lifted their heads and Dave saw their faces darken as they realized they had ridden into the same trap again. The sight of the guns laid on them took some of the starch out of them for a moment, then Sabine snarled: 'There ain't more'n a dozen men up there altogether. We can take 'em.' His voice took on an edgy snap. 'Get Tremaine quick, boys. The rest will fold up when we take him.' Even as he spoke, he reached down for his gun, threw himself to one side in the saddle, and swung the horse around with his free hand so that it stood between him and the bullet which Dave threw at him.

In the same instant, the rest of the gunmen scattered, dropping from their saddles and diving for the boardwalk. Two remained in the saddle, kicked spurs along their horses' flanks, gigging them sharply forward, heading straight for Dave, intent on riding him down. Acting on instinct, he snapped a shot at the first man as he came boring in, saw him reel in the saddle, arching high in the stirrups as the slug took him in the chest. The second rider came on, yelling.

The beating hoofs struck the ground within inches of Dave's head as he went down into the dust, rolling over and over, shielding his head with his arms. He heard the thunder of the hoofs fade along the street as his shoulder hit the bottom of the wooden rails bordering the board-walk. Then everything was drowned out by the gunfire. A window splintered in a tinkling of glass fragments that fell on to the wooden slats near his face. Slugs chopped out strips of wood from the uprights. Frenziedly, he got his legs under him, threw himself up on to the boardwalk, slithered a couple of feet on his belly, then dived for the waterbutt a couple of feet away. A bullet hammered into it within inches of his head and a spout of water splashed on to the boardwalk.

Lex and the others were firing from the roofs and alleys along the street, pouring a hail of fire into the boardwalk that fronted the small store where most of Sabine's men had gone to cover. Corrie and another man scuttled over to Dave.

Breathing heavily as he thrust fresh cartridges into his gun, Corrie said: 'I seen a couple of their men tryin' to sneak out around the side of the store. If we ain't careful, they could sneak out and move around into town, maybe join up some place else.'

Dave studied the terrain. The small grocery store was set by itself, with an alley running along either side of it, back away from the main street. He guessed there would be an open stretch of ground at the back and then a way of getting into one of the other alleys that ran like a veri-table warren in the parts of town that lay away from the main street.

'We've got to get our fire in through the front windows and the door,' he said finally. He looked up and down the street a way. 'Then three men move up near the grain store yonder, take up their positions there where they can shoot along the alley. Two more will have to move further along where they can watch that other side. Reckon you can get them to do that, Lex?'

The other nodded. 'We'll take our Winchesters and plenty of rounds. That way we can chop that place into sawdust.'

'Good. Then get to it. I'll give you coverin' fire from here, wait for you to get into place and then move in from here.'

'You're goin' to try to take 'em from the front?'

'That's the one way they won't be expectin' trouble – through the front door.'

Rapidly conceived, the plan was just as rapidly put into action. Crouching low behind the rain butt, Dave pumped shell after shell into the front of the building. Slugs ripped around him and several times he felt the wind of their passing close to his head, smashing into the woodwork at his back. Corrie and the others gained their positions, although one man was hit as he darted across the street. Dave saw him stagger, go down on one knee, almost dropping his rifle as he did so. Then he pulled himself to his feet and hobbled forward as fast as he could, dropping out of sight beside the rest of the men.

Four men rushed along the boardwalk, heading further along the street to watch the other alley. The first three reached their position without being hit. The fourth, a short, squat man, black-moustached, never made it. The men in the store had seen the first three men, guessed at their intention. They had evidently anticipated the fourth man's move, had been waiting for him to show himself. A shattering hail of fire broke from the windows as he commenced his run, erupting all about him, the force of the leaden slugs driving deep into his body literally picking him up and hurling him back against the boardwalk, where he lay sprawled with sightless eyes turned towards the afternoon sky overhead, arms and legs flung wide.

Lips pressed together in a tight line, Dave sent shot after shot whistling through the smashed windows of the store, heard a man scream from somewhere inside. A vague shape appeared behind one of the windows, half hidden by the jagged splinters of glass still sticking in the frame. Aiming swiftly, he fired again. The man jerked up on tiptoe, pitched forward, head and shoulders smashing through the remaining glass, body hanging halfway out of the window, his fingertips trailing on the wooden slats of the boardwalk.

Waiting for five minutes while the sound of gunfire rose to an ear-splitting crescendo, he loaded his weapon, moved out cautiously from behind the dubious cover of the butt, waited for a moment, crouched down on the edge of the boardwalk, then hurled himself across the street. A couple of slugs kicked up dirt around his legs. At the same moment, a sudden bellow of gunfire to the rear of the store told him that most of the other men had taken up their places there, tangling with any of Sabine's men who might be trying to get away around the rear of the building.

Standing against the wall of the building, the Colt held tightly in his left hand, he edged towards the splintered doorway, moving as quietly as a coyote. He could hear somebody yelling inside, but the voice was muffled and he could not hear the words, nor recognize the voice.

The door looked hard and strong and he felt reasonably sure it would have been locked. It would have been fastened too by a drop bar behind and if that didn't smash with his first blow, then his plan would be finished even before it had begun. Everything depended on breaking down that door at his first try. He would never get a second.

Several bullets had chipped large splinters out of the wood, weakening the door to a certain extent. But he did not have the time to weigh one chance against another. Drawing in a deep breath, bracing himself with the gun held a little away from his body, he moved a foot away from it, judged where the drop bar was likely to be, then hurled his shoulder at the spot with all the strength he could muster. The impact sent a jar of pain stabbing through his right arm, numbing it for several moments. But everything seemed to happen so fast after that there was little time to reflect on the pain. The door cracked loudly, then flew open wide, pitching him sideways into the small room beyond. Ducking low, he brought up the Colt, fired instinctively at the men in the room. Slugs tore through the air near him. Lead plucked at his shirt and jacket. Something burned a red-hot score along his arm. Two men staggered and fell. One slumped over the short counter, face turned sideways, teeth showing through his whiskers.

Dave fired swiftly, without pause, switching targets whenever he saw a man stagger or fall. The room thundered with gunfire. Stabbing flames lit up the darker corners. Several of the gunmen made a rush through the door at the back of the counter, into one of the rooms to the rear, only to be greeted by gunfire there as Corrie and the others moved in.

With the Colt levelled, Dave swung on a tall shape that lifted itself from one corner. The man was struggling to reload his gun in a hurry, the slugs falling on to the floor as his fingers trembled so violently he could scarcely hold them, let alone get them into the chambers of the gun. When he saw Dave advancing on him, the barrel just lining up on his chest, his nerve left him, he dropped the gun with a clatter on to the wooden floor and threw his arms high over his head.

'Don't shoot me in cold blood, Tremaine,' he said whiningly. 'I give in. I quit!'

Slowly, Dave lowered the Colt. 'All right, Sabine,' he said through his teeth. 'Walk out in front of me.'

The other did as he was told, all of the fight knocked out of him. Gunsmoke hung in slowly drifting layers out in the street and there was very little firing. Corrie came out of the store, grinned broadly as he saw Sabine.

'Did you find Forrest in there?' Dave demanded.

The other shook his head. 'I reckon that yeller-livered polecat lit out as soon as he saw his chance.'

Dave tightened his lips. Turning to Sabine, he thrust the barrel of the Colt hard into the small of the other's back. 'Where has Forrest gone, Sabine?' he muttered harshly. 'Either you tell me now, or I'll blow a hole in your back.'

Something in Dave's voice told the other he meant it. Swallowing thickly, he stammered: 'He knows you've guessed he killed your partner, Fordyce. He's gone to make sure that Luke Corrie don't talk.'

'Corrie!' Dave whirled on Lex. 'Keep this *hombre* covered. I'll take care of this.' He began to run along the street in the direction of Doc Keller's surgery, thrusting has way through the crowds of people who had come out now that the shooting was over. Even as he came in sight of the building, he knew he must surely be too late. Forrest would have reached there by now, found Luke lying on the bunk . . .

The gunshot which came from inside the building sounded oddly loud in the stillness that had ensued after the gunfight along the street. Dave increased his gait, jerking the Colt from its holster. The door was open and he was ten feet away when Forest backed through it. Savagely, Dave brought up the gun, intending to call the other out, then lowered the Colt. Forrest was bent over, his legs rubbery. At the edge of the boardwalk his spurs caught in the wood and he fell backwards, hands clutched over his chest, blood oozing between his interlaced fingers. Dave stared in surprise, then glanced up again, Roxanna stepped through the doorway, the smoking gun in her hand still pointed down at the other. There was a faint look of horror on her face. Slowly, Dave went up to her and gently took the gun from her.

'He tried to kill Luke,' she said in a low, hushed voice. 'I had to shoot him. There was nothing else I could do.'

'Everythin' is goin' to be all right now,' Dave said quietly. 'Sabine and his men are finished.'

Lex Corrie came hurrying along the street. He paused for a moment, stared down at the dead body of Forrest lying in the dust, then looked anxiously at Roxanna. She interpreted his glance correctly.

'Luke is all right, Mr Corrie,' she said. 'I'll take you in to him.'

Corrie nodded, started up the steps after her, then paused as he drew level with Dave. He said softly: 'You know, even if the townsfolk don't offer you the Sheriff's job permanently, I figure there'll be plenty of ranches goin' around here now that a man could work if he really put his mind to it.'

'Sure,' Dave smiled faintly. 'Trouble is I've never had any experience handling a ranch before. I wouldn't even know how to start.'

'Virginia knows plenty,' Corrie said. 'I reckon if you was to ride out to the ranch now and have a talk with her, she might agree to help you with a place of your own.' He winked broadly at Dave, then walked into the surgery and closed the door very deliberately behind him.

Dave waited for a moment in the hot sunlight, then made his way quickly to the livery stables. He'd need the fastest horse they had if he was to reach the ranch and Virginia before sundown.

(L)